FREE AGENTS

Also by Max Apple

THE ORANGING OF AMERICA
ZIP

FREE AGENTS

Max Apple

1817

HARPER & ROW, PUBLISHERS, New York

Cambridge, Philadelphia, San Francisco, London

Mexico City, São Paulo, Sydney

A6482f

Portions of this work originally appeared in *The Atlantic, Esquire, Fiction Network, The Iowa Review, The Kenyon Review, Mademoiselle, The Movies, Paris Review, Ploughshares, Texas Stories & Poems,* and *Twentieth Century Literature.*

"Kitty Partners" first appeared in *Antaeus*.

"Carbo-Loading" first appeared in *Junk Food*, by John Farago, Charles J. Rubin, David Rollert, and Jonathan Etra. Published by Dell Publishing Co., Inc., in 1980.

"The American Bakery" first appeared in *The New York Times Book Review* under the title "My Love Affair with English."

"Walt & Will" first appeared in *American Review #26* under the title "Disneyad." Published by Bantam Books, Inc.

"Stranger at the Table" first appeared in *Esquire* under the title "Keeping Kosher."

FIRST EDITION

Designer: Jane Weinberger

Library of Congress Cataloging in Publication Data

Apple, Max.
  Free agents.
  I. Title.
PS3551.P56F7 1984   813'.54   83-48810
ISBN 0-06-015282-6

84 85 86 87 88 10 9 8 7 6 5 4 3 2 1

Several of the pieces in *Free Agents* are obviously biographical; others are not directly connected to my life. I hope this does not confuse anyone. For the record, I do have two children, Jessica and Sam, who are as real as they can be.

To them, I dedicate this book.

Contents

FREE AGENTS

Walt and Will

W alt Disney could watch an ant farm or a beehive with the attention other men gave a football game. He could gaze tirelessly at the tiny, faceless creatures, all leg and antenna, with their chocolate-drop bodies and pinpoints of color. His original idea of the animated cartoon came from the simplest secret of small-creature life: there is no stillness. Life is crawling, creeping, eating, listening, defecating, waiting with a few legs in the air while the footsteps of strangers echo all through your body. From early boyhood, young Walter could pick out specific ants on the farm. He needed no color coding or infrared markers, even if these had been available to him. There were certain characteristics which individualized an ant to him. A dragging of one leg, a birth defect perhaps, a slight discoloration upon an otherwise fine, deep black body. Sometimes it was "personality" that shined forth the individual being, the way a particular ant whom young Walt called Marc would always stop dead in his tracks whenever a flashlight illumined his workday. The curious ant stopped to wonder at the sudden light the way primitive men might have marveled at an eclipse.

Will never shared or even attempted to understand his brother's hobby. If they caught some frogs together Will would try to sell them to fishermen, but it was always Walt's instinct to domesticate them. Walt was fascinated even by the night crawlers which they regularly collected and sold ten for a penny. All that motion under rocks, he thought. "Just jab at the earth anywhere," he told Will, "and you'll see a hundred things coming to life. When you put a shovel into the ground it's like sunrise for the worms."

Will Disney nicknamed his younger brother Birdhead when Walt won the 1916 Turner Street Elementary School Audubon Society award. At eight, Walter could imitate a canary, a parakeet, a sparrow, a starling, and a robin redbreast. Because they had him, the Disney household was devoid of pets. At Will's urging Walter would go through the five-room frame house imitating a different bird in each room. In the basement coal bin, where his practice disturbed nobody, Walt tried out the larger, nonmusical animals: the roar of the jungle beast, the surprisingly mellow tone of the crocodile, the almost silent purr of the domestic cat always beside her master.

Father Disney was a mail carrier who allowed no dog imitations in his household and no noise whatsoever after his 8 P.M. bedtime. Mrs. Disney, tending her house and a small porch garden against the erratic Missouri weather, watched in almost total silence the swift spurt to manhood of her two sons. The Disney boys both lamented the fact that neither parent lived long enough to see Walter's peculiar talent become one of the great ideas of the century. "Constant movement and sound," Walt rambled in an interview years later, "what else is the cartoon?"

Will, who managed all the ventures, even the third-grade Audubon contest, thought the story was the most important element. "You can't just have a damn mouse moving around a screen," he told Walter when he saw and appreciated his brother's first Mickey Mouse frames. "The mouse has to be trying to get something. A cheese, a girlfriend, a job—something." Will's insistence created the earliest version of Minnie, a dowdy gray matron named Pearl whose round form and schoolteacher smile made her less alluring than Will had hoped she would be.

An initial philosophical premise separated the brothers on cartoons throughout their lives. Will wanted tits on Pearl Mouse. "Mice don't have tits," Walt said laconically and refused to draw even the tiniest bulge on his standing matronly mouse as she tied her frilly apron strings and looked at the pies cooling on her mousehole windowsill. To Walt Disney a mouse was always a mouse. You could make him a railroad engineer, a ship's captain, a middle-class husband and father if you wanted to, but a mouse he was still. In the shadow Walter saw the substance, in the movement he perceived the constant. Mouseness, not humanity, was the heart of his creation. The business Disney saw it otherwise. The mouse was only a cute disguise for the man who lurked within. If you put tits on girl mice, then Mickey could walk up and squeeze one and everyone would get a kick out of that, even people who would be surprised or offended to see a human caricature do such a thing on a public screen.

Because Will saw the man where Walter saw the mouse, the early cartoons, the only ones the brothers actually made themselves, had a kind of schizophrenic duality. Will wrote a human script celebrating the continuity of thought and action, Walter drew creatures who in each of their thousand incarnations failed to remember the "self" of their previous drawing. "Mickey was taller than Pearl when they first met," Will would point out to his brother, who had forgotten as he drew the images that the two mice had indeed met and courted and made significant and promising gestures to each other only a few hundred drawings earlier.

To Walt Disney, the cartoon was like the ant farm. You just let your eye wander around the surface. You watched tiny actions, meaningless to you but interesting because of the motion under glass. What was the "story" in the activity under a rock or in a mousehole? His original mouse moved so quickly that Walt drew neither close-ups nor full-face angles for the camera. Mickey had long rodent teeth, dark blotchy fur. He moved around on four legs.

"Jesus Christ," Will Disney said when he delighted in the movement but was appalled by the features, "why is the mouse so damned ugly? Why doesn't he stand up like a man?"

On this phrase, "like a man," Disney Studios in 1932 almost faltered before they began. Walt was twenty-seven and drawing on a splintered easel. He had a studio in a barn outside Kansas City. Will, thirty and married, sold space in a grain elevator to support his bride and gave whatever he could to his dreamy kid brother, who in five years had not held a job beyond three months.

"Like a man," Will Disney said in April 1932, "like a man, or I don't buy you another fucking paintbrush." From April through July, Walt Disney drew no creatures. His easel lay face down amid the strands of straw, his pigments lost their freshness, his brushes hardened. The brothers Disney, all their lives as close as testicles, barely exchanged greetings during these months. Walt took a job with a WPA road crew. At night he was too tired to miss his drawing. He cleaned up, ate, and went to bed. On weekends he picnicked with Lucille Walters, whom he would marry in 1934 but to whom he could not explain in the summer of 1932 why he suddenly stopped the drawings which for years had been his special hobby and were part of the great charm to which Lucille was attracted. He brought her drawings of flowers instead of the real thing, sketches of gifts he would have bought for her if he could.

"Walt Disney," she finally said, "I don't know what's happened between you and Will and maybe it's none of my business, but if you don't stop moping around and go back to your drawing, you can just stop coming around on weekends too."

The loss of Lucille and Will would have been too much. At the end of July 1932, Walt Disney quit his job on the road crew and Mickey Mouse, for the first time, stood up like a man. He drove a steamboat and pulled on the whistle with childish delight. For his brother, Walt named the man-mouse Steamboat Willie. Willie smacked his red humanlike lips at female mice and felt them up in their tight bodiced gowns. The two-footed mouse had ambition greater even than his lust. He longed to be a ship's captain plying his big steamer along the Mississippi, openly blowing his raspy whistle in the ports where his ancestors used to huddle beneath the docks drooling for the remnants of grain. He would not settle, this ballsy mouse, for being like a man, he wanted to be a big man, a leader, one whose actions changed the world, one who roused in women sighs deep enough to move sheets drying on the line. When Steamboat Willie, lunging from his whistle and salivating for big-city life, pulled into New Orleans, ocean liners made way and Creole girls tugged at their petticoats. He made for the waterfront jazz parlors, where respectful mice, dark as the ace of spades, laid oyster stew and shrimp gumbo before this man-mouse bursting with appetite. Barely off his sea legs, Steamboat pulled a lithe waitress to his hot lap and spoon-fed her those squiggly oysters and the down-home gumbo that had put such roses in her cheeks. "Oh, sailor boy," she cooed as his five-fingered mouse hand disturbed layers of crinoline. Not long did the sailor enjoy such bliss. A wart-encrusted first mate in a buccaneer's hat claimed the girl and flattened the ambitious sailor with a hard thump on the head. Walt Disney drew a rainbow for the unconscious mouse, a smooth, curving arc that disappeared into the horizon and suggested opaque colors. Will later made him change it to stars.

The young mouse shook the rainbow from his head and pummeled the brute so mercilessly that the warts fell from the mean sailor's body and formed a small, independent mound that begged in the voices of suffering Negroes for an end to this beating. Steamboat did not stop until the girl rubbed herself against him like a cat. He lowered his fists and raised his passion. The warts jumped back on their man and led him from the tavern. Steamboat and Sweet Sue embraced. He tugged her beneath the oysters, which climbed out of their stew to peer at the sport. On the waterfront, Steamboat's now-quiet ship sat on smooth coastal waters awaiting the success that bloomed beyond even Will Disney's hopes. Steamboat Willie curbed his libido and became the young Mick. Sweet Sue, no longer so easy herself but equally sweet, donned an apron and a more open-mouthed smile to charm the world as faithful Minnie, created in spite of the stubbornness of the creator by the worldly wisdom of his brother. To the applause of all mankind, Walt Disney's mouse had become "like a man," but his creator's vision stayed forever with that long-toothed, four-footed rodent who visited him regularly in the barn. Walt Disney never liked the plots and never cared what happened to the mice. When he gave his final approval to a cartoon he looked only for stillness. His sharp eye could spot a static one-sixteenth of a second. But if an editor were to put Franklin Roosevelt in the frame to replace the mouse, Walt Disney would have approved the plot as automatically as ever.

Because Will's insistence on human styles had unmanned him before his public career even began, Walt Disney took no pleasure in the creatures who bore his name.

He OK'd Donald Duck at a casual luncheon with some draftsmen. Goofy, Pluto, Scrooge, the various deer, squirrels, and elk that sprang from Disney Studios were all committee decisions overseen by Will and later by a marketing specialist. Walt Disney never saw *Dumbo* until its commercial release. Because Walt himself had such prominent ears, Will didn't want to risk offending his brother before release. Perhaps because it was made completely without him, Dumbo became Walt Disney's favorite Walt Disney character.

Once the success started, Will left his brother alone to do as he pleased. Only the name Walt Disney became famous. The man married Lucille Walters and finally moved to Hollywood after World War II when Will said it was getting to be a big public-relations problem for Walt to stay in Missouri. Will chose his brother's house, his car, his wardrobe, and, when it became necessary, even his toupee. The periodic Walt Disney depressions which Will tried to talk him out of had begun to occur almost as soon as Walt drew Steamboat Willie. The brothers loved each other whole-heartedly and Walt was as pleased as Will with most of the fruits of wealth, but he could never overcome his initial belief that mice ought to be as distant from people in cartoons as they were in real life. The success of Disney Studios and later of Disneyland were direct contradictions of this notion. Although after 1934 Will never rubbed it in, each successive Disney enterprise proved conclusively that everybody wanted human-type creatures. Almost alone in the civilized world was the taste of Walt Disney, fascinated by ant farms and aglow over random motion. For love and money he went along with Will on all the Disney ventures. But when Lucille died in 1955, Walt moped more than ever. He preferred to stay at home and draw as he always did the realistic creatures that nobody ever saw in a Disney cartoon. Will came over daily to cajole his brother out of the mansion, to get him to the studio or at least to the Brown Derby for lunch. For Will's sake he went to Orlando, just as for Will's sake he played the part of being uplifted by pep talks. At first it had worked a little, and the smile continued to fool Will over the years. Yet Walt Disney's melancholy had grown almost in proportion to his success. He carried his sadness with him shrouded in his personable, easygoing style so that it almost appeared as an envious ease with the material world. Will brought him ventures, but since Steamboat Willie there had been no "adventures," no risks of his talent, no taste of the world. Walt Disney, lionized and admired since his late twenties, felt at sixty, as he hovered queasy-stomached over Orlando, like a bronze statue in the middle of a small town.

II

In fact, for the cruise over Orlando the Disney brothers made one of their rare changes in itinerary. Usually they did not travel in the same aircraft or even stay at the same hotel. Walt could not leave California without being skeptical about all the past Mickey Mouse business.

"We did the goddamn mouse thing," he said often, "and that's enough. How many goddamn mouse things can a man do?"

Will Disney had the personality to complement his brother's genius. "Walter," he would say, "once you got people listening to a talking mouse you have got them, brother, by the nuts." Will called his brother's creation "Milky Mouse," because he could milk it for all it was worth.

Years after making it big, Walt still had no confidence. Money in the bank did little to bolster him. Becoming an international celebrity only made him think less of the world. "Sometimes I think, Will, that one of these mornings I'm just going to wake up and find out that it's all over. The Mouse, Donald, Pluto, Scrooge, Minnie, the nephews, the comic books, the whole drafting department gone like a flushed toilet."

"Yes," Will said, "but if that ever happens your shoes and your bed and your house and California and New York will all be gone too. When are you going to realize, Walter, that what we have is a product, the same as cars and food and clothes. When are you going to stop whining about Mickey and Donald and wake up to the whole damn industry? Did Henry Ford worry that someday people would stop buying the Model T? The hell he did. For twenty years he wouldn't even give 'em a second color. Do farmers sit around on their butts not planting seed just in case there's going to be a drought next summer? And what about the whole damn clothing industry? On just about any day, people can stop buying new duds and make do for a couple of years. That don't scare the shit out of Seventh Avenue. Hell no, it just makes people work harder, take bigger risks. It keeps things interesting, Walter, and you and I, brother, we're in the most interesting business of all."

Will could always bring him out of the dumps with his little pep talks. He had to remind Walter that they were part of a big, wide, profitable world.

"A few smiles for your brother, Walt. That old silver lining for Will, who remembers changing your diaper. There, that's the Walt Disney everybody loves. Not a moper, not a loser. Remember what Mom used to say, 'Shit smells and class tells'? Goddamn it, Walt, we got 'em by the balls. Who are you worried about, Woody Woodpecker? Lantz hasn't made a decent woodpecker in fifteen years. You worried about TV, about Hanna-Barbera? Shee-it. They go three frames a second—that's not movies, that's stillies. You worried about the banks? Christ, we got up to forty million in credit already cleared with J. P. Morgan. The Bank of America thinks we're a better buy than Warner Brothers. Did you ever think, Walt, back in K.C., that someday you and I would be a better pick than the Warner Brothers, the Marx Brothers, or any goddamn brothers in the world? We're something now, Walt Disney, and don't forget it.

And I'll tell you a secret, brother, we're not breathing hard yet. When Walt Disney, Inc., gets its second wind, just watch us go. General Motors, you better look out for your ass."

"How'd we come outta the same Mom and Dad, Will? We're day and night, the two of us."

"That's why we're winners, brother. Between us we cover all the shots."

Will smoked cigars and slapped backs. Walt gravitated toward corners. "You said the Dodgers would never leave Brooklyn. Walter, remember that, remember when you told me it was crazy to buy so much out here, remember. Well, Walt Disney, if all your movies disappeared like the athlete's foot, you'd still be sitting on a kingdom. This is not mice and ducks. This is *real estate.* It's magic, Walt. I always said fuck the stock market, fuck commodities, get us some land and let every poor bastard come over to have a little fun. You wanna leave it all for those Six Flags phonies? They've got three spots already. They're big with farmers, big in the South, you want peanuts like that to get all the benefit of what we did on the Coast? Face it, Walt. Do you want the real Disneyland or do you wanna let the imitators take it over?

"Sure, I've bought the land, but we can back out. It's not too late, just a few thousand bucks lost. We can plant oranges, tomatoes, anything you want, Walter. I'm not going to force another Disneyland. I thought I'd go under from all your worries before we ever opened in Anaheim. No Tomorrowland, you said, no Frontier City, no Mississippi Steamer. If you'd called the shots, Walter, we'd of had an amusement park like Shelby's where Mom used to take us. And old Walt Disney could stand up on a platform and hand out the teddy bears. When are you gonna realize, Walt, that you're the tops? More kids know the Mouse than Jesus Christ. We could build a religion, a college, an atom-powered village—anything we want. But I say we need another Land, only this time with nothing held back—no nine-watt bulbs this time, no cardboard, no fiberboard. Plywood–glass–steel–aluminum. A railroad, an airport, a hotline the president will be jealous of. We'll be the Statue of Liberty for another planet. In the year 2065, when those men from Mars come down here, and you bet your ass they will, I want 'em to ask first thing, before they wanna know politics and science and all that jazz, I want 'em to ask 'Where's the Disneys' world? We read the lights in the stars and we picked your earth over a dozen other neat places because of Disneyworld.' That's what I want, Walt, and we'll have it, the Lord willing, four and a half years from tomorrow, when we'll float over Orlando like bees on a rose.''

To celebrate the coming of the new world, the brothers Disney, just this once, got in a helicopter together to overlook Orlando. Walt insisted that they wear parachutes. A second company helicopter trailed them in case of any emergency.

Adolph West of the Transpacific Insurance Company, uncomfortable in his parachute, and Virgil Nicolson, representing the Chase Manhattan Bank, accompanied the Disneys. Will couldn't hold back his excitement as they climbed into the twelve-passenger helicopter. He helped the bankers into their genuine leather seats. "Hughes just got a big government order for these for the Army. They strip them down, load 'em with cannons, and pop the commies right out of the trees. In L.A. the talk was about one and a half billion for a three-year contract. We're still punks compared to the military business, aren't we, Adolph?''

The financier nodded in smiling agreement. "Had your Dramamine, Walter?'' Will asked. "OK, let her rip.'' From a secluded corner of a private airfield west of Orlando, the Disneys rose in their two-bladed blue helicopter. Over the palm trees of central Florida, over the occasional elms laid waste by vines creeping up their limbs, over the quiet, lonely, damp streets of Orlando, the Disney helicopters hovered and scanned.

"When we looked at Anaheim,'' Adolph West recalled, "there wasn't this kind of space. It was all oranges and avocados, not a plowed farm or a plain old nonfruit tree anywhere around there. Here it's like upstate New York with a little good weather.''

"Yes,'' Will said, "it cost us a lot less for the acreage here, but it wasn't only the money. You know why I wanted Florida? I wanted it because we're like a belt around the country when we're here and in California. Same latitude, same climate, same kind of people, really: the kind that can't take the big cold cities. Miami is like L.A., too far gone in construction to buy what we need. Now the 'glades would have been good but then you hit the transportation problem in there. I believe I talked to you, Virg, or maybe it was someone else from Chase, about financing a few dozen hovercrafts to wheel the crowds through the swamp. That way we could have turned a nice profit and made it some fun just getting people from one Land to another. But the swamps aren't really deep enough for those big air boats, and someone said to me once, How would it look, Will, if a swamp buggy with about two hundred kids went down in the muck near Never-Never Land? After that you'd have ten years of mothers taking their kids waterskiing and skydiving and being scared shitless of Disneyland.

"So when we shelved the Everglades we started looking inland, and there was Orlando. When I saw it I knew how Columbus must have felt. You couldn't have asked for anything more perfect. Good superhighway, a new airport, dirt-cheap farms full of watermelons and okra. The whole place like a big old plantation with lots of sleepy coons and a few rich masters going to parties in Key West and Miami. It was in '59 when I first saw it and started putting the package together slowly so that nobody would suspect. I didn't even tell you New York people. If the word had been out, every water-melon farmer would have wanted ten times more for his land. No, we waited and it's been better than six years. The land that's left is mainly the big clumps. That fucking mink farmer bought two thousand acres from under our nose; we'll have to do something about him. And then there's a few hundred that some old heiress has and that's about the only big stuff left on the perimeter. Sportsservice, I can tell you, is very interested in the concessions. I think we can clear as much as fifty percent from their gross, and the restaurants and motels, the gas stations and shopping centers will all be after us for space."

"Does it really have to be this big?" Adolph West asked. "Virgil and I were both thinking about the same size as Anaheim might be enough."

Will chuckled. "You boys are just like Walt, you just can't stand to think a little beyond right this minute. How many people are there in the country, Adolph; about two hundred million, right? And more than half are kids, and three quarters of their parents have enough extra cash to take two-week vacations and send the kids to camp. And there's also about one million Japs and Turks and Frenchmen and others coming to Anaheim every year right now. What we're planning is roughly three times the size of Anaheim, and I guarantee you that by 1980, maybe sooner, we'll wish it was three times that.

"Look at Walt. Sure he seems creepy and airsick this minute, but Walt could have stopped thirty years ago and still been the most successful artist in the history of the world. You know I get a kick now and then out of these art books talking about Michelangelo or Leonardo or some other Italian making their pictures seem like the people could really move. Hell, Walter and the boys in the drafting room are making people and animals that move sixty-three times a second and in color. And they do it mostly with their hands and their eyes and a pen just like the old-timers did. Suppose someone had told Michelangelo that, five hundred years from now, Walt Disney Studios could take that whole Vatican ceiling which damn near broke his neck, put it all on celluloid, add as much color as it needs, and make the whole thing *move*. The hand of God *moves* right over to Adam's hand and shakes it. The breath of God *moves* right into the body of Adam. I've been talked out of religious cartoons by everybody, but I've thought for years that there's a market there right in those same Sunday schools whose ministers keep telling me it would be sacrilegious. If it's not sacrilegious to have the saints and the apostles and everybody in the picture books, why is it a sin to put them into Disney cartoons? Nobody's answered that one for me yet, but who wants to mess with the Pope?

"What if we made just one as an experiment, showing, say, the loaves and the fishes or Jesus on the water, nothing sad or bloody, just some well-known miracle? I'd say one good seven-minute cartoon that we could put out for less than eighty thousand would revolutionize the Sunday schools."

Adolph West seemed as interested in the religious films as in the new Disneyland. "I believe you have something there, Will. I don't see anything irreligious about making the Gospels in fine, tasteful children's versions."

Will liked to impress the bankers with his ideas. After all, it was his ideas and their money that made everything happen right from the start. "Well, Adolph, if you think I've got something, see if you can put a little heat on Bishop Sheen or Billy Graham or some of the big shots in the National Council of Churches. A few years ago, one of our creative men did go to Bishop Sheen with some terrific sketches. Jesus looked just like he always does. He was wearing a white toga with a rope belt and a pair of two-thousand-year-old sandals that we actually had made by a guy in L.A. so that our artists could watch a foot move in those old-fashioned things. They were goatskin. I mean, for the walking on the water you need some real close-ups of the feet. And you know the best effect of all and the easiest is this incredible glow you can get around his head just by leaving some white space on a specially treated paper. I mean it was really something. We spent about twenty-five thousand just on the preparation and the sketches. We talked to Stravinsky about the music and Vincent Price for the voice, but the Bishop said, 'No dice.' And this George Beverly Shea who does all the Billy Graham arrangements said it was too cute. Imagine a guy like him calling Walt Disney and Stravinsky too cute. Did anyone say De Mille's *Ten Commandments* was too cute? No, they didn't, but if it had been Walt Disney Presents *The Ten Commandments,* you can bet your ass the church would have been on our neck. De Mille has the reputation for handling big productions, and everyone thinks we can't do anything more serious than Mickey Mouse.

"Well, Adolph, you learn to do what you can in this world. The churchmen won't let us bring the saints to Sunday school, but they'll pack those kids into chartered buses and drive them a thousand miles to see a cardboard Jesse James rob a cardboard train and shoot up some plastic people. I can't figure it out, so I say, let's give 'em what they want. Right, Walter?

"How ya doin' back there?" In the rear of the helicopter Walt

Disney lay upon three seats folded for him into a soft couch in the row behind his brother and the two bankers.

"I'm doing OK, Will. When we get over the territory, let me know and I'll get up. I'm sure it's going to be OK, but I don't want to take any chances by sitting up too soon."

Will could talk, Will could deal. He could plan the sparkling future. Because of Will, Walt's sketches had taken life. Animation techniques made the characters move in the eye of the camera, but Walt Disney knew it was his brother's determination that actually moved Walt Disney, Inc., and the millions of drawn animals therein.

There was no reason to argue when he knew that Will was right. This new place would probably be even better than Anaheim, and that one had made all their earlier achievements seem like the minor leagues. It took something to risk it all on one idea. If Disneyland hadn't made it big, the whole studio would have collapsed with it. But even though they made it, somehow Walt was sorry they had done it.

"I like the movies. I like the drawings," he told Will, when the original idea came to his older brother one night at the studio bowling alley. "Let's stick with what we like. You're talking about buildings and mechanics and bonds and stuff we don't know about."

Will sparkled like Tinker Bell and waved his magic hand. "Man is only dust and time and spirit," Will said, "but Disneyland can make him strong as an angel." He threw a strike, scattering the pins deep into the abyss. "Look at us, Walt, we've got Rolex watches and Bel Air mansions, Rolls-Royces, and kids at Harvard, and still, Walt, there's more to it than what we've taken out. We've made people happy, haven't we? Who would you say has made more fun for more people, the Disney brothers or Shakespeare? Who has done more good, the Disneys or Queen Elizabeth and Harry Truman and Woodrow Wilson and all the politicians combined? We're not doing it for us, big Walter, it's for them. They need a place to take the kids. Where can a mom and pop in this great country go with the little ones? Oh, they can go for a picnic in the country with a thousand bugs or a dull ball game with a hundred drunks in the bleachers. The old man can't keep up with the kids in any of the games they play, and he hates their records and their friends.

"When we were kids, Walt, where'd we want to go, remember? You wanted to go see the Mormon temple in Utah, and I wanted to see the Washington Monument. Maybe kids still want to see the nation's capital, I don't know, but if you had a choice now of laying out a lot of money for the White House or a place in California where you could enjoy the rides and the restaurants and the walks as much as the kids do, where would you go?"

Bowling pins were flying all around them. Walt just held his twelve-pound ball by three fingers while his brother went on about Disneyland, which was taking shape right there in lane number 11.

"I guess I'd go to Disneyland," Walt admitted, "but I wish someone else would build it."

Will motioned him to the seats behind the scorer's table. "Until this second, Walter, I never realized that America does not have her own national monument. Think about it. England's got dozens of places everybody has to see, France has the caves, the Riviera, the wine making. What did we skip over to India for, the Taj Mahal, right? Up to this minute, Walter, America has no spot that you have to see, and every rinky-dink country in Europe and around the world has one. We'll build a center for America. A place where you can stand and move the world from."

A ragged old pinsetter stuck his head out from behind the bowling lane's facade. "Hey, I ain't got all night. Are you fuckers gonna roll one or not?"

Walt Disney, powerless as usual before the brilliant energy of his brother, picked up his Brunswick Black Beauty and, aiming toward Anaheim, rolled one effortlessly down the middle.

Bridging

At the Astrodome, Nolan Ryan is shaving the corners. He's going through the Giants in order. The radio announcer is not even mentioning that by the sixth the Giants haven't had a hit. The K's mount on the scoreboard. Tonight Nolan passes the Big Train and is now the all-time strikeout king. He's almost as old as I am and he still throws nothing but smoke. His fastball is an aspirin; batters tear their tendons lunging for his curve. Jessica and I have season tickets, but tonight she's home listening and I'm in the basement of St. Anne's Church watching Kay Randall's fingertips. Kay is holding her hands out from her chest, her fingertips on each other. Her fingers move a little as she talks and I can hear her nails click when they meet. That's how close I'm sitting.

Kay is talking about "bridging"; that's what her arched fingers represent.

"Bridging," she says, "is the way Brownies become Girl Scouts. It's a slow steady process. It's not easy, but we allow a whole year for bridging."

Eleven girls in brown shirts with red bandannas at their neck are

16

imitating Kay as she talks. They hold their stumpy chewed fingertips out and bridge them. So do I.

I brought the paste tonight and the stick-on gold stars and the thread for sewing buttonholes.

"I feel a little awkward," Kay Randall said on the phone, "asking a man to do these errands . . . but that's my problem, not yours. Just bring the supplies and try to be at the church meeting room a few minutes before seven."

I arrive a half hour early.

"You're off your rocker," Jessica says. She begs me to drop her at the Astrodome on my way to the Girl Scout meeting. "After the game, I'll meet you at the main souvenir stand on the first level. They stay open an hour after the game. I'll be all right. There are cops and ushers every five yards."

She can't believe that I am missing this game to perform my functions as an assistant Girl Scout leader. Our Girl Scout battle has been going on for two months.

"Girl Scouts is stupid," Jessica says. "Who wants to sell cookies and sew buttons and walk around wearing stupid old badges?"

When she agreed to go to the first meeting, I was so happy I volunteered to become an assistant leader. After the meeting, Jessica went directly to the car the way she does after school, after a birthday party, after a ball game, after anything. A straight line to the car. No jabbering with girlfriends, no smiles, no dallying, just right to the car. She slides into the back seat, belts in, and braces herself for destruction. It has already happened once.

I swoop past five thousand years of stereotypes and accept my assistant leader's packet and credentials.

"I'm sure there have been other men in the movement," Kay says, "we just haven't had any in our district. It will be good for the girls."

Not for my Jessica. She won't bridge, she won't budge.

"I know why you're doing this," she says. "You think that because I don't have a mother, Kay Randall and the Girl Scouts will help me. That's crazy. And I know that Sharon is supposed to be like a mother too. Why don't you just leave me alone."

Sharon is Jessica's therapist. Jessica sees her twice a week. Sharon and I have a meeting once a month.

"We have a lot of shy girls," Kay Randall tells me. "Scouting brings them out. Believe me, it's hard to stay shy when you're nine years old and you're sharing a tent with six other girls. You have to count on each other, you have to communicate."

I imagine Jessica zipping up in her sleeping bag, mumbling good night to anyone who first says it to her, then closing her eyes and hating me for sending her out among the happy.

"She likes all sports, especially baseball," I tell my leader.

"There's room for baseball in scouting," Kay says. "Once a year the whole district goes to a game. They mention us on the big scoreboard."

"Jessica and I go to all the home games. We're real fans."

Kay smiles.

"That's why I want her in Girl Scouts. You know, I want her to go to things with her girlfriends instead of always hanging around with me at ball games."

"I understand," Kay says. "It's part of bridging."

With Sharon the term is "separation anxiety." That's the fastball, "bridging" is the curve. Amid all their magic words I feel as if Jessica and I are standing at home plate blindfolded.

While I await Kay and the members of Troop 111, District 6, I eye St. Anne in her grotto and St. Gregory and St. Thomas. Their hands are folded as if they started out bridging, ended up praying.

In October the principal sent Jessica home from school because Mrs. Simmons caught her in spelling class listening to the World Series through an earphone.

"It's against the school policy," Mrs. Simmons said. "Jessica understands school policy. We confiscate radios and send the child home."

"I'm glad," Jessica said. "It was a cheap-o radio. Now I can watch the TV with you."

They sent her home in the middle of the sixth game. I let her stay home for the seventh too.

The Brewers are her favorite American League team. She likes Rollie Fingers, and especially Robin Yount.

"Does Yount go in the hole better than Harvey Kuenn used to?"

"You bet," I tell her. "Kuenn was never a great fielder but he could hit three hundred with his eyes closed."

Kuenn is the Brewers' manager. He has an artificial leg and can barely make it up the dugout steps, but when I was Jessica's age and the Tigers were my team, Kuenn used to stand at the plate, tap the corners with his bat, spit some tobacco juice, and knock liners up the alley.

She took the Brewers' loss hard.

"If Fingers wasn't hurt they would have squashed the Cards, wouldn't they?"

I agreed.

"But I'm glad for Andujar."

We had Andujar's autograph. Once we met him at a McDonald's. He was a relief pitcher then, an erratic right-hander. In St. Louis he improved. I was happy to get his name on a napkin. Jessica shook his hand.

One night after I read her a story, she said, "Daddy, if we were rich could we go to the away games too? I mean, if you didn't have to be at work every day."

"Probably we could," I said, "but wouldn't it get boring? We'd have to stay at hotels and eat in restaurants. Even the players get sick of it."

"Are you kidding?" she said. "I'd never get sick of it."

"Jessica has fantasies of being with you forever, following baseball or whatever," Sharon says. "All she's trying to do is please you. Since she lost her mother she feels that you and she are alone in the world. She doesn't want to let anyone or anything else into that unit, the two of you. She's afraid of any more losses. And, of course, her greatest worry is about losing you."

"You know," I tell Sharon, "that's pretty much how I feel too."

"Of course it is," she says. "I'm glad to hear you say it."

Sharon is glad to hear me say almost anything. When I complain that her $100-a-week fee would buy a lot of peanut butter sandwiches, she says she is "glad to hear me expressing my anger."

"Sharon's not fooling me," Jessica says. "I know that she thinks drawing those pictures is supposed to make me feel better or something. You're just wasting your money. There's nothing wrong with me."

"It's a long, difficult, expensive process," Sharon says. "You and Jessica have lost a lot. Jessica is going to have to learn to trust the world again. It would help if you could do it too."

So I decide to trust Girl Scouts. First Girl Scouts, then the world. I make my stand at the meeting of Kay Randall's fingertips. While Nolan Ryan breaks Walter Johnson's strikeout record and pitches a two-hit shutout, I pass out paste and thread to nine-year-olds who are sticking and sewing their lives together in ways Jessica and I can't.

II

Scouting is not altogether new to me. I was a Cub Scout. I owned a blue beanie and I remember very well my den mother, Mrs. Clark. A den mother made perfect sense to me then and still does. Maybe that's why I don't feel uncomfortable being a Girl Scout assistant leader.

We had no den father. Mr. Clark was only a photograph on the living room wall, the tiny living room where we held our monthly meetings. Mr. Clark was killed in the Korean War. His son John was in the troop. John was stocky but Mrs. Clark was huge. She couldn't sit on a regular chair, only on a couch or a stool without sides. She was the cashier in the convenience store beneath their apartment. The story we heard was that Walt, the old man who owned the store, felt sorry for her and gave her the job. He was her landlord too. She sat on a swivel stool and rang up the purchases.

We met at the store and watched while she locked the door; then we followed her up the steep staircase to her three-room apartment. She carried two wet glass bottles of milk. Her body took up the entire width of the staircase. She passed the banisters the way semi trucks pass each other on a narrow highway.

We were ten years old, a time when everything is funny, especially fat people. But I don't remember anyone ever laughing about Mrs. Clark. She had great dignity and character. So did John. I didn't know what to call it then, but I knew John was someone you could always trust.

She passed out milk and cookies, then John collected the cups and washed them. They didn't even have a television set. The only decoration in the room that barely held all of us was Mr. Clark's picture on the wall. We saw him in his uniform and we knew he died in Korea defending his country. We were little boys in blue beanies drinking milk in the apartment of a hero. Through that aura I came to scouting. I wanted Kay Randall to have all of Mrs. Clark's dignity.

When she took a deep breath and then bridged, Kay Randall had noticeable armpits. Her wide shoulders slithered into a tiny rib cage. Her armpits were like bridges. She said "bridging" like a mantra, holding her hands before her for about thirty seconds at the start of each meeting.

"A promise is a promise," I told Jessica. "I signed up to be a leader, and I'm going to do it with you or without you."

"But you didn't even ask me if I liked it. You just signed up without talking it over."

"That's true; that's why I'm not going to force you to go along. It was my choice."

"What can you like about it? I hate Melissa Randall. She always has a cold."

"Her mother is a good leader."

"How do you know?"

"She's my boss. I've got to like her, don't I?" I hugged Jessica. "C'mon, honey, give it a chance. What do you have to lose?"

"If you make me go I'll do it, but if I have a choice I won't."

Every other Tuesday, Karen, the fifteen-year-old Greek girl who lives on the corner, babysits Jessica while I go to the Scout meetings. We talk about field trips and how to earn merit badges. The girls giggle when Kay pins a promptness badge on me, my first.

Jessica thinks it's hilarious. She tells me to wear it to work.

Sometimes when I watch Jessica brush her hair and tie her ponytail and make up her lunch kit I start to think that maybe I should just relax and stop the therapy and the scouting and all my not-so-subtle attempts to get her to invite friends over. I start to think that, in spite of everything, she's a good student and she's got a sense of humor. She's barely nine years old. She'll grow up like everyone else does. John Clark did it without a father; she'll do it without a mother. I start to wonder if Jessica seems to the girls in her class the way John Clark seemed to me: dignified, serious, almost an adult even while we were playing. I admired him. Maybe the girls in her class admire her. But John had that hero on the wall, his father in a uniform, dead for reasons John and all the rest of us understood.

My Jessica had to explain a neurologic disease she couldn't even pronounce. "I hate it when people ask me about Mom," she says. "I just tell them she fell off the Empire State Building."

III

Before our first field trip I go to Kay's house for a planning session. We're going to collect wildflowers in East Texas. It's a one-day trip. I arranged to rent the school bus.

I told Jessica that she could go on the trip even though she wasn't a troop member, but she refused.

We sit on colonial furniture in Kay's den. She brings in coffee and we go over the supply list. Another troop is joining ours so there will be twenty-two girls, three women, and me, a busload among the bluebonnets.

"We have to be sure the girls understand that the bluebonnets they pick are on private land and that we have permission to pick them. Otherwise they might pick them along the roadside, which is against the law."

I imagine all twenty-two of them behind bars for picking bluebonnets and Jessica laughing while I scramble for bail money.

I keep noticing Kay's hands. I notice them as she pours coffee, as she checks off the items on the list, as she gestures. I keep expecting her to bridge. She has large, solid, confident hands. When she finishes bridging I sometimes feel like clapping the way people do after the national anthem.

"I admire you," she tells me. "I admire you for going ahead with Scouts even though your daughter rejects it. She'll get a lot out of it indirectly from you."

Kay Randall is thirty-three, divorced, and has a Bluebird too. Her older daughter is one of the stubby-fingered girls, Melissa. Jessica is right; Melissa always has a cold.

Kay teaches fifth grade and has been divorced for three years. I am the first assistant she's ever had.

"My husband, Bill, never helped with Scouts," Kay says. "He was pretty much turned off to everything except his business and drinking. When we separated I can't honestly say I missed him; he'd never been there. I don't think the girls miss him either. He only sees them about once a month. He has girlfriends, and his business is doing very well. I guess he has what he wants."

"And you?"

She uses one of those wonderful hands to move the hair away from her eyes, a gesture that makes her seem very young.

"I guess I do too. I've got the girls and my job. I'm lonesome, though. It's not exactly what I wanted."

We both think about what might have been as we sit beside her glass coffeepot with our lists of sachet supplies. If she was Barbra Streisand and I Robert Redford and the music started playing in the background to give us a clue and there was a long close-up of our lips, we might just fade into middle age together. But Melissa called for Mom because her mosquito bite was bleeding where she scratched it. And I had an angry daughter waiting for me. And all Kay and I had in common was Girl Scouts. We were both smart enough to know it. When Kay looked at me before going to put alcohol on the mosquito bite, our mutual sadness dripped from us like the last drops of coffee through the grinds.

"You really missed something tonight," Jessica tells me. "The Astros did a double steal. I've never seen one before. In the fourth they sent Thon and Moreno together, and Moreno stole home."

She knows batting averages and won-lost percentages too, just like the older boys, only they go out to play. Jessica stays in and waits for me.

During the field trip, while the girls pick flowers to dry and then manufacture into sachets, I think about Jessica at home, probably beside the radio. Juana, our once-a-week cleaning lady, agreed to work on Saturday so she could stay with Jessica while I took the all-day field trip.

It was no small event. In the eight months since Vicki died I had not gone away for an entire day.

I made waffles in the waffle iron for her before I left, but she hardly ate.

"If you want anything, just ask Juana."

"Juana doesn't speak English."

"She understands, that's enough."

"Maybe for you it's enough."

"Honey, I told you, you can come; there's plenty of room on the bus. It's not too late for you to change your mind."

"It's not too late for you either. There's going to be plenty of other leaders there. You don't have to go. You're just doing this to be mean to me."

I'm ready for this. I spent an hour with Sharon steeling myself. "Before she can leave you," Sharon said, "you'll have to show her that you can leave. Nothing's going to happen to her. And don't let her be sick that day either."

Jessica is too smart to pull the "I don't feel good" routine. Instead she becomes more silent, more unhappy looking than usual. She stays in her pajamas while I wash the dishes and get ready to leave.

I didn't notice the sadness as it was coming upon Jessica. It must have happened gradually in the years of Vicki's decline, the years in which I paid so little attention to my daughter. There were times when Jessica seemed to recognize the truth more than I did.

As my Scouts picked their wildflowers, I remembered the last outing I had planned for us. It was going to be a Fourth of July picnic with some friends in Austin. I stopped at the bank and got $200 in cash for the long weekend. But when I came home Vicki was too sick to move and the air conditioner had broken. I called our friends to cancel the picnic; then I took Jessica to the mall with me to buy a fan. I bought the biggest one they had, a 58-inch oscillating model that sounded like a hurricane. It could cool 10,000 square feet, but it wasn't enough.

Vicki was home sitting blankly in front of the TV set. The fan could move eight tons of air an hour, but I wanted it to save my wife. I wanted a fan that would blow the whole earth out of its orbit.

I had $50 left. I gave it to Jessica and told her to buy anything she wanted.

"Whenever you're sad, Daddy, you want to buy me things." She put the money back in my pocket. "It won't help." She was seven years old, holding my hand tightly in the appliance department at J. C. Penney's.

I watched Melissa sniffle even more among the wildflowers, and I pointed out the names of various flowers to Carol and JoAnne and Sue and Linda and Rebecca, who were by now used to me and treated me pretty much as they treated Kay. I noticed that the Girl Scout flower book had very accurate photographs that made it easy to identify the bluebonnets and buttercups and poppies. There were also several varieties of wild grasses.

We were only 70 miles from home on some land a wealthy rancher long ago donated to the Girl Scouts. The girls bending among the flowers seemed to have been quickly transformed by the colorful meadow. The gigglers and monotonous singers on the bus were now, like the bees, sucking strength from the beauty around them. Kay was in the midst of them and so, I realized, was I, not watching and keeping score and admiring from the distance but a participant, a player.

JoAnne and Carol sneaked up from behind me and dropped some dandelions down my back. I chased them; then I helped the other leaders pour the Kool-Aid and distribute the Baggies and the name tags for each girl's flowers.

My daughter is home listening to a ball game, I thought, and I'm out here having fun with nine-year-olds. It's upside down.

When I came home with dandelion fragments still on my back, Juana had cleaned the house and I could smell the taco sauce in the kitchen. Jessica was in her room. I suspected that she had spent the day listless and tearful, although I had asked her to invite a friend over.

"I had a lot of fun, honey, but I missed you."

She hugged me and cried against my shoulder. I felt like holding her the way I used to when she was an infant, the way I rocked her to sleep. But she was a big girl now and needed not sleep but wakefulness.

"I heard on the news that the Rockets signed Ralph Sampson," she sobbed, "and you hardly ever take me to any pro basketball games."

"But if they have a new center things will be different. With Sampson we'll be contenders. Sure I'll take you."

"Promise?"

"Promise." I promise to take you everywhere, my lovely child, and then to leave you. I'm learning to be a leader.

Small Island Republics

nudo was probably the world's tallest Japanese-American. Six-five-and-a-half barefoot, he also had extra measures of Oriental cunning and agility. He was good at basketball and paper folding. He honored his parents and got all A's at Harvard, where he majored in American history. He was twice voted the Japanese-American teenager of the year and went around the country giving after-dinner speeches to fourteen-year-olds who wanted, someday, to be like him. Young Japanese girls swooned as if he were Mick Jagger when he told them that their parents had been put in prison camps in California. They admired his silky complexion and his deep rich voice reading racist tracts of the '30s and '40s in which San Fernando Valley farmers accused the Japanese of pissing on their lettuce.

"You've got to be aware of the fact that some of your neighbors still think of you as the yellow menace," he told the youngsters. They took notes and asked for his autograph.

It bothered young Inudo to hear Japanese-Americans talk about "the homeland." "My homeland is California, U.S.A.," he said. He rode along the scenic Route 1 on his two-cycle Suzuki with a short-throw engine. In polished knee-length boots, leather jacket, and cycling helmet, Inudo looked like a kamikaze pilot. He liked to talk in generalizations. Hannibal of Carthage was his hero. The Japanese-American Citizens League voted him a trip to Japan, including a ceremonial meeting with the prime minister.

Inudo refused the trip. "When will you start believing that you're full American citizens?" he bellowed to his young audiences. "When will you stop thinking that it's kind of our hosts to keep us here? My great-grandfather was born in California, and they still imprisoned my father during the war in case he was an alien spy."

"Forget the war," his father told him. "I forgot, the Japanese forgot, the Germans forgot. You weren't even born until 1956. If you want to talk about old wars, stick with your Hannibal and the Romans."

Inudo's mother wanted him to be a senator. Even a state senator would do. "Look at B. S. Hirahimo," she urged him, "Daniel Iawahara, Victor Benawara." She knew the names of Japanese elected personages down to the county level. "You could be a justice of the peace next week," she said, "if you'd just stop talking silliness." Senator Hirahimo himself nominated Inudo to be a page in the U.S. Senate.

"Let them use computers more effectively," he said, turning down the job. "The hand-carried message is as obsolete as the Morse code."

He liked to gun his Suzuki through downtown San Jose. The wind in his wake lifted skirts. People watched the tall handsome Oriental vanish uphill, his chrome tailpipes smoking.

"A year out of Harvard and still nothing," his mother complained. "You turn down what others dream about." Gradually, and much less radically than other Americans his age, Slim Inudo stopped honoring his parents.

"Why do I have to be something?" he asked. "Why can't I be Slim Inudo of San Jose and work for one of the local conglomerates? Why in the hell don't you get off my back?"

Stress, the senior Inudos thought. Too many A's, too much of an idol. Who at fifteen and sixteen should be held up as an example to strangers? "I'm sorry," Mrs. Inudo moaned to her husband, "that I taught him the Bill of Rights at age three. I trained him to be a credit to his people and he was. And now at twenty-two he's retired."

Inudo began dating a Caucasian coed from San Jose State. She could be seen clutching him from behind astride the Suzuki. She studied journalism and wanted someday to edit the newspaper in her Iowa hometown. She had light brown curls and kept a stenographer's notebook tucked in her jacket. She met Inudo when she interviewed him for the college newspaper. She admired his honesty in the face of journalistic pressure.

"I don't like it," Mrs. Inudo said. "A Caucasian girl, a Jane Somebody from Iowa. I was sure he would marry one of our own."

"Jesus Christ," Inudo said, "she is our own. My grandparents were in California when hers were still in Ireland."

"Look, Mr. Historian," the senior Inudo said, "we know the facts too. I don't want you to talk that way to your mother."

Inudo apologized. "The world is in turmoil," he said. "We recognize China, lose Iran, run a great risk of a national economic catastrophe, and all you worry about is the pigmentation of my girlfriend's skin."

"The color of her skin is history," Mrs. Inudo said.

Her son pulled on his boots.

"Mom and Dad . . ." he said. Years as an orator had taught him dramatic pause. He read the anguish in their faces. "I hate to do this, but I'm twenty-three now." The hope of the next generation moved into Caucasian Jane's student apartment.

Pressed for cash and feeling independent, Inudo hired on as a security guard for the Taiwanese Trade Office in San Jose. The presence of such a large Oriental made the trade officials feel less betrayed. He played gin rummy with them. With the Taiwanese, Inudo could generalize about Carthage, Atlantis, ancient Tyre and Babylon. They identified and felt the pangs of the ancient suffering.

"All will be lost for us too," the Taiwanese said. Their fatalism made them erratic card players, and Inudo won more than his salary.

"The Eastern nations should form an OPEC of the electronics

industry," he urged. "Governments are only figureheads. Real power has already shifted to transnational economic blocs. Taiwan, Korea, and Hong Kong can put the squeeze on textiles too. Fight back," he urged. "Don't be like my father, who is not angry about being in an American prison camp when he was a teenager."

The Taiwanese liked his spunk. They hated Jimmy Carter more than Inudo hated the memory of Franklin Roosevelt. Beside Inudo as he ginned on the Taiwanese legates, Jane felt as if she were in the presence of the significant. She bought him a long cashmere scarf that tickled her ears when she sat behind him on the Suzuki.

H. L. Lee, the San Jose liaison, introduced Inudo to Huey "Bo" Huang, Taiwan's main man in world trade. Huang, a beaten man, stopped in San Jose on his way home after failing to even get an interview with the Assistant Secretary of Commerce. A wise man even in defeat, Huang marveled at the surprising size of Slim Inudo. "A regular Wilt Chamberlain," he said.

"Don't patronize me," Slim Inudo said. "The stakes are high for your small island republic. There is no time for idle talk."

Bo Huang knew a good man when he saw one. Huang's father was related on both sides of his family to General Chiang Kai-shek. Genetics, thus, made Huang a diplomat; by inclination he preferred American sports, light reading, and the company of small-boned women.

Slim Inudo found the American abandonment of Taiwan the first great issue of his adult political life. He was too young for Vietnam, but betrayal by the West was his favorite theme.

"Woe to those who trusted in Rome," he told Huang, "and woe to the small island republic that is less than self-sufficient." He mentioned Mytilene in the Aegean Sea at the time of the Peloponnesian Wars.

"Listen," Bo Huang said over a half cup of oolong tea, "I'm on my way back to Taipei after a rough forty-eight hours in D.C. Give me a break." Bo took off his shoes and watched the office gin game.

Slim Inudo in his tan Burns security uniform looked like a Boy Scout troopmaster when on the office blackboard he outlined the major political issues of the day. Bo Huang sucked on his pipe. "A thinker like you is always useful in government," he said. "Unfortunately we Taiwanese are now cutting back on employment. No longer will we maintain full consulates throughout the world." He looked sadly at H. L. Lee and the San Jose boys. He shook his head. The gloom made Jane shiver. Slim Inudo ginned and the San Jose boys pulled out their dollars.

"It sounds abstract to most Americans," Lee said. "They can't tell one Chinaman from another. And Vietnam confused them so much they curtailed the domestic production of globes. When Americans look east they want to see what Marco Polo saw."

"Marco Polo," Inudo said, "was a popularizer, a trivializer. He was like the astronauts who go to the moon to play golf."

Huey "Bo" Huang smiled in amazement. "You should be at the UN."

"That's what my mother says."

Jane stroked Inudo's long dark hair and peeked over his shoulder at the gin rummy hand.

"Your mother," Huang said, "knows personnel."

Inudo smiled and dropped his cards. "Listen, fellas," he pleaded, "don't give up. Taiwan is already off the front pages, but it will be an issue for years. Lots of Americans are with you. I am, and I'm as far from Ronald Reagan as you can get. It has nothing to do with power politics. It's a matter of small island republics."

Huang shook his head sadly. "You're a good boy, Slim, but we didn't become the free world's largest textile mill by forgetting realism. No, we won't go the way of Jonestown or Masada, nor will the hunchbacked pinkos ever drink our blood. We'll just curl up and die of loneliness." Small tears rolled quickly down Mr. Huang's round cheeks. Jane reached in her purse for Kleenex. The San Jose trade mission boys scuffed their shoes and looked away from one another.

Slim Inudo said, "I'm sick of this saving-face business. You guys may be Orientals; I'm an American." He went to the phone and called Washington.

Slim Inudo's name was well known among the Washington staff of Senator B. S. Hirahimo. Some still bristled over Slim's abrupt refusal to become a page after high school. All of them knew of his recent forays into Caucasian girls and the generation gap. Mrs. Inudo wrote monthly letters to the senator. The senator himself had given her the idea. When she received his monthly "Report from Washington" she decided that if the senator had the time, so did she. "The Inudo Report" reached his desk on the first of each month. His staffers jokingly put it on the top of his pile of work whenever it arrived. The name "Inudo" became in the Hirahimo office a synonym for small-town mentality. They called Jimmy Carter an Inudo. Kings and princes, governors and various federal agency directors were called either first-class or second-class Inudos. Someone from the staff thanked Mrs. Inudo each month for her report.

When Slim telephoned from the Taiwanese Trade Office, the secretary merely announced an Inudo calling. They all thought it was an Inudo from Consumer Affairs or Environmental Protection or Defense. An Inudo with the Taiwanese, a genuine Inudo, was a major diplomatic event. They paged Hirahimo from the Senate floor, where he was reading last month's *Intellectual Digest*. The senator was not as fond of the Inudo joke as his staffers were. He treated the call from Slim as a serious complaint from a constituent. He said that he too was disturbed by the Taiwanese about-face.

"When a man like Huey Huang can't even get a ten-minute appointment with the Assistant Secretary of Commerce, someone's looking up the wrong hole," Slim said. He was an Inudo who never minced his words.

"I'll see what I can do," the senator promised.

"I'll wait for your call," Slim said. "I'll be at this number until five."

Huey "Bo" Huang, dabbing at his cheeks with Jane's Kleenex, said, "With a few dozen like you we wouldn't need recognition from the rest of America."

Emily Inudo never knew how instrumental her monthly reports were in her son's sudden reawakening to civic duty. "One day he's moving in with a plain Jane," she said to the senior Inudo, "the next he's going to Washington with the Taiwan ambassador. Genius can't stay hidden for too long." The elder Inudos stored his Suzuki in the garage and promised to keep the chrome parts free of rust.

Jane bought her own half-fare ticket and accompanied him. "It's not just romance," she told the skeptical Inudos. "I'm a journalist, and this may be a major story."

Emily Inudo could overlook the girlfriend. Her son was finally on his way to Washington. "When he comes back," she told her husband, "he'll have a title. I know it."

Senator Hirahimo called Commerce and made an appointment for Huey Huang of the Republic of China. "It's just kind of an embarrassment," Commerce told the senator, "to have these Taiwan people hanging around. I mean, the ax fell. You'd think they'd turn their embassy into a townhouse or something and stop dry cleaning their flags."

The senator stood firm. By four o'clock he called Slim Inudo and gave him a date and appointment time. On the spot Huey "Bo" Huang hired Slim as a Washington lobbyist for the Republic of China.

Slim Inudo turned in his Burns security outfit for a three-piece Hong Kong suit. The tailor whistled through his teeth when he measured Inudo's inseam. "That's one Texas-size Jap," he said.

"An American," Slim Inudo corrected, "a one-hundred-percent American of Oriental lineage."

Huey Huang insisted on ordering three suits for Slim. "Expense account," he said. "Washington is a dress-up city." Jane bought a shirtwaist, two pairs of low-heeled shoes, and a strapless gown. Mr. Huang put it on the tab. "You're judged by your company too." He threw in a new hairdo from Saks Fifth Avenue. "When you're representing a government, personal expenses don't mean anything," he said. "You have to think in larger terms."

An Air Taipei charter refueling in Oakland carried them first class to Washington. For Jane and Slim it was their first trip to the nation's capital. The charter was taken up by Filipinos and by Americans returning from Guam. The Taiwanese were already staying home in great numbers. Stunned and unsure of what to do next, they hoarded canned goods and awaited word on the future of their small island republic.

"We're desperate," Mr. Huang told Inudo. Jane took notes. "We're desperate and the U.S., our friend and ally, is turning her back on thirty years of friendship."

"We'll see about that," Slim Inudo said. Secure in the company of his new employee, Huey Huang relaxed for the first time since the change in the mainland wall posters.

Official Washington hardly noticed the new lobbyist. One more cup of bottomless coffee at the Mayflower Hotel, another pair of ninety-dollar shoes, a few appointments with underlings, extra sales of mimeo paper . . . it happened every day.

Jane and Huey "Bo" Huang knew this was different. "A single man has always been able to affect the course of events," Huang said. "Look at Simón Bolívar, Fidel Castro, Charles de Gaulle, Sun Yat-sen." At Commerce, where Huang wanted to talk textiles, he was told to keep a low profile and not press the Carter administration. "I know you fellas can't see things from our point of view," the Assistant Secretary told Huang, "but we've got a peck of trouble on our hands. Taiwan hasn't been a serious issue since Eisenhower. It's time for everyone to look toward the twenty-first century."

Huang cabled his government in code, H BOMB ONLY HOPE.

"I could stay here," he confessed to Slim and Jane at dinner. "I could do very well for myself. Lots of governments would hire me as a trade consultant, and IBM has made me a most attractive offer. My salary now is peanuts by comparison."

"You cannot put a price on patriotism," Slim said. "That tiny island republic needs you. The venture capitalists of the West have a host of MBA programs."

"Don't I know it," Huang said, fighting bitterness. "Haven't I lectured at Harvard, Pennsylvania, Cornell, Stanford, and UCLA, breaking up a busy schedule time and again to give tips on international business free of charge."

"You should know," Inudo said, "that the European always has and always will continue to think of us as an oddity. My own projection for the next two hundred years is for renewed and bitter Muslim-Christian wars. The Orient will become the world's only sanctuary, with Russia and India joining the religious wars."

Jane took it all down. Columnists at nearby tables chewed lightly and ordered their waiters to stand still until Slim finished his statement. Scattered applause rang through the Sans Souci.

"But in the meantime," Huang said, "in the short run, in the next five or ten years, what can we do?"

"Arm to the teeth," Inudo said. "Hire mercenaries and sign mutual defense pacts with every unaligned nation."

"Come now," said an unnamed high State Department official from a secluded table at the rear. "That will only lead to total ostracism. We are still your friends. Only geopolitical events have brought us to this temporary misunderstanding about national identity and territorial aspiration."

There was much applause. "Let's get out of here," Inudo said. "I heard that in D.C. you had to watch your tongue, but I didn't expect this."

"It was worse during Watergate," Huang said. "Then everyone was routinely taping small talk. You could never flag a waiter. They were always running out to buy AA batteries for someone important. A Taiwanese engineer solved the problem with an inexpensive and portable voice-actuated device. Nobody in Washington even asked his name."

"The faceless," Inudo said, "the fodder of history." He rose and signed for his dinner. "If they look to the twenty-first century, so can we."

The existence of small republics coincided with the attention to size that was the graph of Slim Inudo's life. He was twelve to fifteen inches taller than any of his relatives. To Inudo love meant, early on, bending and restraint of power. He felt sometimes like a bird or animal magically able to understand human speech. In his extra-long trousers and size 15 shoes he went with his father to shop in the boys' department. He was big, very big, but he felt small and he understood smallness. In crowds he suffocated even when his head bobbed above everyone else's. To his family he was a freak of nature but they felt blessed by his awesomeness, aware of the special responsibility of such an offspring. Emily Inudo likened her big boy to Samson and worried about his fate among the Philistines. When his father took two-year-old Slim for his first haircut, Emily cried all day. She told her husband her ideas about Samson for, already at two, his height soared off the growth charts.

"Well, then it's better for me to take him for a haircut than his girlfriends," the senior Inudo joked, but as the boy continued to grow past the size of all their known ancestors he too began to suspect a special destiny for young Slim.

They never had to caution the boy about gentleness to his peers. On the playground he deferred to everyone. Even in high school as a star basketball forward he made his reputation on defense and gladly let others take the shots. Emily Inudo saw no hint of a Delilah in Jane Williams. There was no exoticism of dress or manner, no femaleness lying in wait with a scissors; just a very pretty brown-haired girl long from knee to hip and aware of her blue-green eyes.

Although he had moved from their household in the spirit of youthful rebelliousness, their Slim wrote long letters from Washington explaining his preoccupation with Taiwan.

"The world," he wrote, "is in its penultimate stages of a transference from the last gasps of capitalism. Marxism too is fading like the 1920s. The future of political and social development really lies with the small republics. It was Athens, not Persia or even Rome, that gave us our ideologies, and Marxism has its best chance in a place like Cuba. If only the big powers would let the small republics develop independently, the world might know real progress."

"Does he belong in Congress," Emily Inudo asked her husband, "or doesn't he?" She sent copies of certain of his letters to Senator Hirahimo.

Jane, too energetic for simple housekeeping, found a part-time job with the Associated Press. She suspected that the CIA, aware of Inudo's work and anxious to eavesdrop, somehow got her the job.

"It was so easy," she said. "No transcript, no portfolio, an interview full of smiles, and nine dollars an hour, set your own schedule. It's not like the real world is supposed to be."

Mr. Huang did not take her suspicions seriously. "The CIA is treacherous," he admitted, "but not as powerful as a beautiful woman. Beauty always sets its own hours."

Jane blushed. "Not at SJ State it didn't." Her work put her in instant touch with world events. Anything remotely connected to Taiwan she clipped and stuck in her purse. But the news ran entirely to the mainland. A few senators from rural areas wrote letters of condolence to the Taiwan embassy, but no longer could Huey "Bo" Huang talk about the Republic of China without confusing people.

Delegations from the Chinese mainland to the U.S. became routine. When Coca-Cola signed a long-term agreement with Peking, Taiwan's nervous citizens, not trusting in the Hong Kong black market, began to hoard Coke. Their government and the Coca-Cola company tried to reassure them, but siege mentality was everywhere. In two weeks you couldn't find a Coke on the island. Jane put a story on the AP wire about the Coke shortages, but no paper ran it. Instead the media covered the endless jaunts of Peking officials to prison rodeos, barbecues, and midnight dinners in Hollywood.

"Siege mentality is not exciting news," Slim Inudo said. "You see that it's glamour alone that brings attention."

"I would have never believed it," Jane said. "In the classroom we are so isolated that it hurts."

Inudo and Jane huddled beside the fireplace of their Georgetown apartment planning the future of small island republics. Huang had established an office for Inudo at the embassy, but Slim preferred to work at home. He registered as a representative of a foreign government, reported his salary, and claimed only himself as a deduction. In "The Inudo Report" Emily called her son a "goodwill ambassador," but in his heart malign calculation dwelled. He read history for many hours each day.

"I thought," Mr. Huang said finally, "after your exuberant success in obtaining an interview with the Commerce Department that you might work at a less leisurely pace." Bo Huang, a desperate man, did not want to offend Inudo but his small island republic showed daily signs of export slippage.

"There is no immediate hurry," Slim said after reading intelligence estimates from the Defense Department. "Your population is not in danger, and there is no critical shortage of raw material. The people of the island are unified. They will triumph. I am studying options."

"We have experts and our own State Department," Huang said. "Don't try to shoulder the burden completely, just do a little public relations."

Inudo closed the covers of *Capitalism and Material Life: 1400–1800* and put a long arm around his employer. "Bo," he said, "let's get it straight. You know I'm thinking of much more than a contract or two. If I'd wanted to hawk wares I could have gone to law school or become a professional Japanese-American. I want to develop a policy for small island republics. It's not just Taiwan. There are the tourist jewels of the Caribbean, there is Madagascar, the Azores, even Israel, a tiny island republic in a sea of Arabs. Everywhere the big eat the small. It may be pure physics, the whole universe as hungry as gravity. I want small island republics to maintain their identity. I want no more Carthages, no more teeth sown in the ground of a destroyed landscape, no more Mytilenes abandoned by her trading partners, no more Pearl Harbors on quiet Sunday mornings."

Bo Huang shook his head. "I see what you're saying," he said. "The vista is too grand for my humble capacities. Essentially, I'm a salesman. Statesmanship blinds me." He buried his face in Inudo's sleeve.

"Salesmen are not superfluous," Inudo said, calming his employer. "Whatever else they do, small island republics will always need salesmen. The landlocked nation can be smug, brutal, and self-sufficient. The big can be indifferent. But small island republics create civilization."

Jane stayed patient as her tall Japanese lover buried himself in policy. She worked, cooked four-egg omelettes, made sure the FM classical station didn't fade too badly, and gave Bo Huang reports on Slim's long study and seclusion.

"He's up to something," she told Bo. "He's working day and night, but it's nothing that he'll talk about. He trusts me but I think his ideas are still unformed. He'll tell you as soon as he's got something."

Bo Huang looked at Jane's gleaming complexion. She wore loneliness like an earring. "It must be hard for you," he said.

Jane tried a half smile. "I don't complain." Bo Huang appreciated her well-formed ankles and the slope of her instep as a pennyloafer dangled at the top of her foot.

"It's odd how we are thrown together," he said, "the way big destinies gobble up small ones." He removed Jane's loafer and put the ball of her foot on his knee. Her toes contracted and dug their pattern into his gray silk suit. "I was raised by important people to think of myself as an important person," Huang said. "It's hard to accept the insignificance of one's homeland. Personal relations may be all that we're left with."

When Bo pulled at her anklet Jane crumpled into his lap. "If he had paid me the slightest attention . . ." she moaned.

"I know, I know," the trade ambassador said. "Living in chaotic times has made us all animals."

"If small island republics can't survive," Jane gasped, "is there any hope for personal morality?"

Slim Inudo saw the flowers and the notes, and he read the look in both their eyes. He said nothing, nor did he vary his intense study of documentary and social history. "Personal fidelity means nothing to him," Bo Huang said. "He is a giant, truly a giant, not in body alone."

Jane wondered what her parents would think: first a Japanese-American, then a Chinese trade envoy. *I guess the East is my destiny,* she wrote. Her family was very impressed by the AP job. Her young brother liked the autographed pictures she sent him of all the members of the Senate. *His walls are lined with politicians,* her mother wrote. *His friends come over and quiz each other about who's the senator from where. It's a wonderful way to study civics.*

Inudo regularly sent requests to the Library of Congress. Since he asked on behalf of a foreign trade consulate, he received same-day messenger delivery of whatever he wanted. The Georgetown apartment looked like a library storage room: UN reports, geography textbooks, stories of fabled Atlantis, books everywhere Jane stepped. Only the kitchen remained neat. When Jane was certain he had finished with a stack of materials she took them back to the library herself. But no matter how much she returned, his requests were ever greater. Inudo stopped taking meals with her. He ate in his study at the bay window overlooking P Street.

"I don't know," Bo Huang said to Jane, "but whatever happens we have each other. Maybe that's all destiny ever intended. Maybe Taiwan existed only for you and me to share these moments."

Jane loved his boyish romanticism. On his desk were photos of a wife and three children in front of a white stone mansion in Taipei. "Yes," he said, "nobody lives without obstacles, but I believe in the power of human affection."

Inudo began to make phone calls to California. He also sent telegrams to all parts of the world. After months of solitude he came out of his study and said he needed a secretary and a very secure telephone line. Huey "Bo" Huang had already given up on Inudo and happily settled for Jane. The sudden burst of activity made him nervous. He was enjoying the status quo. Inudo withered him with a glance. The secretary, a discreet Chinese male, moved into the spare bedroom.

Normalization with China progressed so smoothly that Taiwan became as obscure as the Spanish-American War. Only the CIA still seemed interested. Sometimes Jane knew she was being followed as she walked down Pennsylvania Avenue. She did not feel threatened. On windy nights she covered her typewriter and felt extra good knowing the government was watching her as she walked through unsafe neighborhoods to her apartment, where three Oriental men awaited her. The secretary spent all his time typing, Bo cooked, and Inudo talked on the phone and read. Jane felt as if she were living a fairytale with Charlie Chan and his sons. All this intrigue, she thought, all this mystery. She could hardly believe that only a few months ago she was writing term papers and going out with boys. Her work was exciting, her men more exciting still. At her doorstep she threw a kiss to the invisible CIA and the deities that had led her to the nation's capital in times like these.

Inudo, now and then, left the apartment. He never told Jane where he went, and on two occasions he was gone overnight. Bo, who paid the bills, said there were trips to California. If not for Jane the trade ambassador would long ago have fired his large Japanese-American lobbyist. After Inudo's second trip to California and six months without any visible work, Huang in embarrassment told his superior, Ambassador V. V. Fong, that he was going to fire the only remaining trade lobbyist for lack of lobbying.

Fong shook his finger and wagged his head. "No, no, no," he said, "no, no, no." Huey realized that the matter was over his head and never mentioned it again. If whatever Inudo was doing met with the ambassador's approval, Huang need not feel responsible. Textile sales firmed up, and, recognized or not, the Republic of China went ahead with her national life.

When the news broke in the *Washington Post,* Jane sobbed and pounded the pillow. "He could have given me the story," she cried. "He could have told me last night and handed me a Pulitzer Prize. This is how he got even."

Huey "Bo" Huang called Taiwan for confirmation. He shook his head in disbelief. "It's true," he said. "Of course all of the contracts are subject to a vote of the people, but in our country that will be automatic."

In California the Disney executives were very subdued. They spoke about their responsibilities to the population and the need to go slowly. The best legal minds had approved the principle. "A small island republic is as individual as a corporation," Inudo said. "When

I realized that, the rest was simple matchmaking. The Disneys get a highly trained work force and a prime site adjacent to the world's largest populated area. Taiwan, a no-man's land, becomes a Disneyland. What bananas are to so-called banana republics, electronics is to Disneyland. It was a match made in heaven."

The surprised administration legally had no power to interfere with the long-term lease of an island to a corporation. "Of course," Inudo said, "there is no absolute security, the Communists might still attack, but historically communism is uncomfortable with tourism, uneasy with ease. And who could attack an unarmed magical kingdom?" he said. "This small island republic by its merger with a corporate identity might be truly leading the way to the twenty-first century."

After the noon news conference, Inudo granted Jane a private three-hour interview. It was his going-away present. "I didn't keep it from you on purpose," he said. "It was not my choice to let the *Post* break the story."

"I understand," she said. "This interview and all the background stories will get me by-lines for a month." He packed for home and kissed tenderly the now experienced journalist.

Emily Inudo, seeing her son's picture on the front page, raised her joyful eyes to the heavens. "Samson destroyed," she mumbled, "Slim creates. A small island republic is just a start. Someday he'll be a senator."

The Eighth Day

was always interested in myself, but I never thought I went back so far. Joan and I talked about birth almost as soon as we met. I told her I believed in the importance of early experience.

"What do you mean by early?" she asked. "Before puberty, before loss of innocence?"

"Before age five," I said.

She sized me up. I could tell it was the right answer.

She had light-blond hair that fell over one eye. I liked the way she moved her hair away to look at me with two eyes when she got serious.

"How soon before age five?" She took a deep breath before she asked me that. I decided to go the limit.

"The instant of birth," I said, though I didn't mean it and had no idea where it would lead me.

She gave me the kind of look then that men would dream about if being men didn't rush us so.

With that look Joan and I became lovers. We were in a crowded restaurant watching four large goldfish flick their tails at each other in a display across from the cash register. There was also another couple, who had introduced us.

Joan's hand snuck behind the napkin holder to rub my right index finger. With us chronology went backwards. Birth led us to love.

II

Joan was twenty-six and had devoted her adult life to knowing herself.

"Getting to know another person, especially one from the opposite gender, is fairly easy." She said this after our first night together. "Apart from reproduction it's the main function of sex. The biblical word 'to know' someone is exactly right. But nature didn't give us any such easy and direct ways to know ourselves. In fact, it's almost perverse how difficult it is to find out anything about the self."

She propped herself up on an elbow to look at me, still doing all the talking.

"You probably know more about my essential nature from this simple biological act than I learned from two years of psychoanalysis."

Joan had been through Jung, Freud, LSD, philosophy, and primitive religion. A few months before we met, she had re-experienced her own birth in primal therapy. She encouraged me to do the same. I tried and was amazed at how much early experience I seemed able to remember, with Joan and the therapist to help me. But there was a great stumbling block, one that Joan did not have. On the eighth day after my birth, according to the ancient Hebrew tradition, I had been circumcised. The circumcision and its pain seemed to have replaced in my consciousness the birth trauma. No matter how much I tried, I couldn't get back any earlier than the eighth day.

"Don't be afraid," Joan said. "Go back to birth. Think of all experience as an arch."

I thought of the golden arches of McDonald's. I focused. I howled. The therapist immersed me in warm water. Joan, already many weeks past her mother's postpartum depression, watched and coaxed. She meant well. She wanted me to share pain like an orgasm, like lovers in poems who slit their wrists together. She wanted us to be as content as trees in the rain forest. She wanted our mingling to begin in utero.

"Try," she said.

The therapist rubbed Vaseline on my temples and gripped me gently with Teflon-coated kitchen tongs. Joan shut off all the lights and played in stereo the heartbeat of a laboring mother.

For thirty seconds I held my face under water. Two rooms away a tiny flashlight glowed. The therapist squeezed my ribs until I bruised. The kitchen tongs hung from my head like antennae. But I could go back no farther than the hairs beneath the chin of the man with the blade who pulled at and then slit my tiny penis, the man who prayed and drank wine over my foreskin. I howled and I gagged.

"The birth canal," Joan and the therapist said.

"The knife," I screamed, "the blood, the tube, the pain between my legs."

Finally we gave up.

"You Hebrews," Joan said. "Your ancient totems cut you off from the centers of your being. It must explain the high density of neurosis among Jewish males."

The therapist said that the subject ought to be studied, but she didn't think anyone would give her a grant.

I was a newcomer to things like primal therapy, but Joan had been born for the speculative. She was the Einstein of pseudo-science. She knew tarot, phrenology, and metaposcopy the way other people knew about baseball or cooking. All her time was spare time except when she didn't believe in time.

When Joan could not break down those eight days between my birth and my birthright, she became, for a while, seriously anti-Semitic. She used surgical tape to hunch my penis over into a facsimile of precircumcision. She told me that smegma was probably a healthy secretion. For a week she cooked nothing but pork. I didn't mind, but I worried a little about trichinosis because she liked everything rare.

Joan had an incredible grip. Her older brother gave her a set of

Charles Atlas Squeezers when she was eight. While she read, she still did twenty minutes a day with each hand. If she wanted to show off, she could close the grip exerciser with just her thumb and middle finger. The power went right up into her shoulders. She could squeeze your hand until her nipples stood upright. She won spending money arm wrestling with men in bars. She had broken bones in the hands of two people, though she tried to be careful and gentle with everyone.

I met Joan just when people were starting to bore her, all people, and she had no patience for pets either. She put up with me, at least at the beginning, because of the primal therapy. Getting me back to my birth gave her a project. When the project failed and she also tired of lacing me with pork, she told me one night to go make love to dark Jewesses named Esther or Rebecca and leave her alone.

I hit her.

"Uncharacteristic for a neurotic Jewish male," she said.

It was my first fight since grade school. Her hands were much stronger than mine. In wrestling she could have killed me, but I stayed on the balls of my feet and kept my left in her face. My reach was longer so she couldn't get me in her grip.

"I'll pull your cock off!" she screamed and rushed at me. When my jab didn't slow her, I hit her a right cross to the nose. Blood spurted down her chin. She got one hand on my shirt and ripped it so hard she sprained my neck. I hit her in the midsection and then a hard but openhanded punch to the head.

"Christ killer, cocksucker," she called me, "wife beater." She was crying. The blood and tears mingled on her madras shirt. It matched the pattern of the fabric. I dropped my arms. She rushed me and got her hands around my neck.

"I must love you," I said, "to risk my life this way."

She loosened her grip but kept her thumbs on my jugular. Her face came down on mine, making us both a bloody mess. We kissed amid the carnage. She let go, but my neck kept her fingerprints for a week.

"I'd never kill anyone I didn't love," she said. We washed each other's faces. Later she said she was glad she hadn't pulled my cock off.

After the fight we decided, mutually, to respect one another more. We agreed that the circumcision was a genuine issue. Neither of us wanted it to come between us.

"Getting to the bottom of anything is one of the great pleasures of life," Joan said. She also believed a fresh start ought to be just that, not one eight days old.

So we started fresh and I began to research my circumcision. Since my father had been dead for ten years, my mother was my only source of information. She was very reluctant to talk about it. She refused to remember the time of day or even whether it happened in the house or the hospital or the synagogue.

"All I know," she said, "is that Reb Berkowitz did it. He was the only one in town. Leave me alone with this craziness. Go swallow dope with all your friends. It's her, isn't it? To marry her in a church you need to know about your circumcision? Do what you want; at least the circumcision is one thing she can't change."

Listening in on the other line, Joan said, "They can even change sex now. To change the circumcision would be minor surgery, but that's not the point."

"Go to hell," my mother said and hung up. My mother and I had not been on good terms since I quit college. She is closer to my two brothers, who are CPAs and have an office together in New Jersey. But, to be fair to my mother, she probably wouldn't want to talk about their circumcisions either.

From the United Synagogue Yearbook which I found in the library of Temple Beth-El only a few blocks from my apartment I located three Berkowitzes. Two were clearly too young to have done me, so mine was Hyman J., listed at Congregation Adath Israel, South Bend, Indiana.

"They all have such funny names," Joan said. "If he's the one, we'll have to go to him. It may be the breakthrough you need."

"Why?" my mother begged, when I told her we were going to South Bend to investigate. "For God's sake, why?"

"Love," I said. "I love her, and we both believe it's important to know this. Love happens to you through bodies."

"I wish," my mother said, "that after eight days they could cut the love off too and then maybe you'd act normal."

South Bend was a three-hundred-mile drive. I made an appointment with the synagogue secretary to meet Hyman Berkowitz late in the afternoon. Joan and I left before dawn. She packed peanut butter sandwiches and apples. She also took along the portable tape recorder so we could get everything down exactly as Berkowitz remembered it.

"I'm not all that into primal therapy anymore," she said as we started down the interstate. "You know that this is for your sake, that even if you don't get back to the birth canal this circumcision thing is no small matter. I mean, it's almost accidental that it popped up in primal; it probably would have affected you in psychoanalysis as well. I wonder if they started circumcising before or after astrology was a very well-developed Egyptian science. Imagine taking infants and mutilating them with crude instruments."

"The instruments weren't so crude," I reminded her. "The ancient Egyptians used to do brain surgery. They invented eye shadow and embalming. How hard was it to get a knife sharp, even in the Bronze Age?"

"Don't be such a defensive Jewish boy," she said. "After all, it's your pecker they sliced, and at eight days too, some definition of the age of reason."

For people who are not especially sexual, Joan and I talk about it a lot. She has friends who are orgiasts. She has watched though never participated in group sex.

"Still," she says, "nothing shocks me like the thought of cutting the foreskin of a newborn."

III

"It's no big deal," Berkowitz tells us late that afternoon. His office is a converted lavatory. The frosted glass windows block what little daylight there still is. His desk is slightly recessed in the cavity where once a four-legged tub stood. His synagogue is a converted Victorian house. Paint is peeling from all the walls. Just off the interstate we passed an ultramodern temple.

"Ritual isn't in style these days," he tells Joan when she asks about his surroundings. "The clothing store owners and scrap dealers have put their money into the Reformed. They want to be more like the goyim."

"I'm a goy," Joan says. She raises her head proudly to display a short straight nose. Her blond hair is shoulder length.

"So what else is new?" Berkowitz laughs. "Somehow, by accident, I learned how to talk to goyim too." She asks to see his tools.

From his desk drawer he withdraws two flannel-wrapped packets. They look like place settings of sterling silver. It takes him a minute or two to undo the knots. Before us lies a long thin pearl-handled jackknife.

"It looks like a switchblade," Joan says. "Can I touch it?" He nods.

She holds the knife and examines the pearl handle for inscriptions. "No writing?"

"Nothing," says Berkowitz. "We don't read knives."

He takes it from her and opens it. The blade is as long as a Bic pen. Even in his dark office the sharpness glows.

"All that power," she says, "just to snip at a tiny penis."

"Wrong," says Berkowitz. "For the shmekel I got another knife. This one kills chickens."

Joan looks puzzled and nauseated.

"You think a person can make a living in South Bend, Indiana, on newborn Jewish boys? You saw the temple. I've got to compete with a half dozen Jewish pediatricians who for the extra fifty bucks will say a prayer too. When I kill a chicken, there's not two cousins who are surgeons watching every move. Chickens are my livelihood. Circumcising is a hobby."

"You're cute," Joan tells him.

H. Berkowitz blushes. "Shiksas always like me. My wife worries that someday I'll run off with a convert. You came all this way to see my knife?" He is a little embarrassed by his question.

I try to explain my primal therapy, my failure to scream before the eighth day.

"In my bones, in my body, all I can remember is you, the knife, the blood."

"It's funny," Berkowitz says, "I don't remember you at all. Did your parents make a big party, or did they pay me a little extra or something? I don't keep records, and believe me, foreskins are nothing to remember."

"I know you did mine."

"I'm not denying. I'm just telling you it's not so special to me to remember it."

"Reverend," Joan says, "you may think this is all silly, but here is a man who wants to clear his mind by reliving his birth. Circumcision is standing in the way. Won't you help him?"

"I can't put it back."

"Don't joke with us, Reverend. We came a long way. Will you do it again?"

"Also impossible," he says. "I never leave a long enough piece of foreskin. Maybe some of the doctors do that, but I always do a nice clean job. Look."

He motions for me to pull out my penis. Joan also instructs me to do so. It seems oddly appropriate in this converted bathroom.

"There," he says, admiringly. "I recognize my work. Clean, tight, no flab."

"We don't really want you to cut it," Joan says. "He just wants to relive the experience so that he can travel back beyond it to the suffering of his birth. Right now your circumcision is a block in his memory."

Berkowitz shakes his head. I zip my fly.

"You're sure you want to go back so far?"

"Not completely," I admit, but Joan gives me a look.

"Well," Berkowitz says, "in this business you get used to people making jokes, but if you want it, I'll try. It's not like you're asking me to commit a crime. There's not even a rabbinic law against pretending to circumcise someone a second time."

IV

The recircumcision takes place that night at Hyman Berkowitz's house. His wife and two children are already asleep. He asks me to try to be quiet. I am lying on his dining room table under a bright chandelier.

"I'd just as soon my wife not see this," Berkowitz says. "She's not as up to date as I am."

I am naked beneath a sheet on the hard table.

Berkowitz takes a small double-edged knife out of a torn and stained case. I can make out the remnants of his initials on the case. The instrument is nondescript stainless steel. If not for his initials, it might be mistaken for an industrial tool. I close my eyes.

"The babies," he says, "always keep their eyes open. You'd be surprised how alert they are. At eight days they already know when something's happening."

Joan puts a throw pillow from the sofa under my head.

"I'm proud of you," she whispers. "Most other men would never dare to do this. My instincts were right about you." She kisses my cheek.

Berkowitz lays down his razor.

"With babies," he says, "there's always a crowd around, at least the family. The little fellow wrapped in a blanket looks around or screams. You take off the diaper and one-two it's over." He hesitates. "With you it's like I'm a doctor. It's making me nervous, all this talking about it. I've been a mohel thirty-four years and I started slaughtering chickens four years before that. I'm almost ready for Social Security. Just baby boys, chickens, turkeys, occasionally a duck. Once someone brought me a captured deer. He was so beautiful. I looked in his eyes. I couldn't do it. The man understood. He put the deer back in his truck, drove him to the woods, and let him go. He came back later to thank me."

"You're not really going to have to do much," Joan says, "just relive the thing. Draw a drop of blood, that will be enough: one symbolic drop."

"Down there there's no drops," Berkowitz says. "It's close to arteries; the heart wants blood there. It's the way the Almighty wanted it to be."

As Berkowitz hesitates, I begin to be afraid. Not primal fear but very contemporary panic. Fear about what's happening right now, right before my eyes.

Berkowitz drinks a little of the Manischewitz wine he has poured for the blessing. He loosens his necktie. He sits down.

"I didn't have the voice to be a cantor," he says, "and for sure I wasn't smart enough to become a rabbi. Still, I wanted the religious life. I wanted some type of religious work. I'm not an immigrant, you know. I graduated from high school and junior college. I could have done lots of things. My brother is a dentist. He's almost assimilated in White Plains. He doesn't like to tell people what his older brother does.

"In English I sound like the Mafia, 'a ritual slaughterer.'" Berkowitz laughs nervously. "Every time on the forms when it says Job Description, I write 'ritual slaughterer.' I hate how it sounds."

"You've probably had second thoughts about your career right from the start," Joan says.

"Yes, I have. God's work, I tell myself, but why does God want me to slit the throats of chickens and slice the foreskins of babies? When Abraham did it, it mattered; now, why not let the pediatricians mumble the blessing, why not electrocute the chickens?"

"Do you think God wanted you to be a dentist," Joan asks, "or an insurance agent? Don't be ashamed of your work. What you do is holiness. A pediatrician is not a man of God. An electrocuted chicken is not an animal whose life has been taken seriously."

Hyman Berkowitz looks in amazement at my Joan, a twenty-six-year-old gentile woman who has already relived her own birth.

"Not everyone understands this," Berkowitz says. "Most people when they eat chicken think of the crust, the flavor, maybe of Colonel Sanders. They don't consider the life of the bird that flows through my fingers."

"You are indeed a holy man," Joan says.

Berkowitz holds my penis in his left hand. The breeze from the air conditioner makes the chandelier above me sway.

"Do it," I say.

His knife, my first memory, I suddenly think, may be the last thing I'll ever see. I feel a lot like a chicken. I already imagine that he'll hang me upside down and run off with Joan.

She'll break your hands, I struggle to tell him. You'll be out of a job. Your wife was right about you.

The words clot in my throat. I keep my eyes shut tightly.

"I can't do it," Berkowitz says. "I can't do this, even symbolically, to a full-grown male. It may not be against the law; still, I consider it an abomination."

I am so relieved I want to kiss his fingertips.

Joan looks disappointed but she, too, understands.

"A man," Hyman Berkowitz says, "is not a chicken."

I pull on my trousers and give him gladly the fifty-dollar check that was to have been his professional fee. Joan kisses his pale cheek.

The holy man, clutching his cheek, waves to us from his front porch. My past remains as secret, as mysterious, as my father's baldness. My mother in the throes of labor is a stranger I never knew. It will always be so. She is as lost to me as my foreskin. My penis feels like a blindfolded man standing before the executioner who has been saved at the last second.

"Well," Joan says, "we tried."

On the long drive home Joan falls asleep before we're out of South Bend. I cruise the turnpike, not sure of whether I'm a failure at knowing myself. At a roadside rest stop to the east of Indiana beneath a full moon, I wake Joan. Fitfully, imperfectly, we know each other.

"A man," I whisper, "is not a chicken." On the eighth day I did learn something.

Child's Play

My children and I have come to Dallas, but we're here looking for the new Hollywood. Our cab driver is from Haiti. He points out the grand buildings of Dallas and suggests that we stop at any one of them. All have mirrored exteriors. We keep seeing ourselves as we circle through the city. After about an hour the driver admits that he doesn't know where the new Hollywood is. He says he doesn't even know where the old one is.

We know that it's somewhere near Dallas, and that it's called Las Colinas. Finally, a gas station attendant suggests that we try the Prairie of the Minor Arts. We drive past the sun-bleached bones of chefs and photographers, past the monuments to papier-mâché and the Whittling Hall of Fame, and there, in a mesquite wilderness, we find a brand-new movie studio. It looks like Hollywood must have looked to the conquistadores as they tramped over the Pacific foothills, Hollywood in the days before the missions turned quaint, before all the Indians had names like Chief Kiss My Tochis.

It also looks like a studio on the moon. It's just off Luna Road and is surrounded by pockmarked craters. The only sign of human life is a band of condominiums huddled near the horizon for a blink at the world but already curving back into darkness.

Though the landscape looks bleak for human habitation, this new Hollywood is paradise for animals. Across the road from the Las Colinas studio is a stable with the dimensions of a Grand Hotel. It costs $1,800 a month to board your mount here, in a style that would satisfy Leona Helmsley if she were a horse.

In the distance, from the swamp near the condos, we can hear the twang of Texas gondoliers as they ply the new canals that connect the new hotels to the new malls to the new Texans and their new money.

I explain to Jessica and Sam that, in the movie business, where you are doesn't matter as long as you convince people that the background is authentic. The time, however, is pretty important. Sam presses my digital watch to check the year and we enter the studio very sure of time, a little hazy about place. The director likes it this hazy; he wants a lot of confusion. He wants a little plot and some background noise—"punctuation," he calls it, but confusion is the most essential ingredient. When you have that the rest will just happen. When you have the right confusion you can drink and gamble and hang around waiting for the money to come in. The actors will act, the cameraman will point the camera, about ninety hours of film will emerge as surely as prayers are uttered in Iran.

When the children and I arrive, the director is celebrating his fiftieth birthday. He wears a golf cap and has a white goatee. He's happy with his birthday, happy with the confusion, some of which he's creating, some of which he'll film, but most of it he can't film because it takes place upstairs in the office, not downstairs on the set.

He's a little overweight, a little out of the limelight, a little broke, a little stoned, but he's all there, and he's large, larger than Dallas. He welcomes us, delighted to have a bit more confusion, a writer and two children to join his actors, his production crew, his wife and family, his drinking buddy, and his stagehands.

After wandering around the studio for a half hour my son says, "So this is what Hollywood is like." Sam is seven. It's the first time he's been around a movie production.

"It's not Hollywood," I remind him, "it's Dallas." But he has made an honest mistake. He has watched a young actor turn a lighted cigarette into his mouth with a flick of his tongue; he has seen the director and the crew begin a spontaneous high-stakes poker game, gathering suddenly around an empty desk like children gathering to play marbles; he has met an accountant who is writing a novel about seventeenth-century India; he has met a former hockey player and a former football player; and he has seen a Teamsters picketer sit down to gossip with the Democratic party's arch prankster. And all this happened in the office—we haven't seen the sound stage yet. There is also a producer, a lot of whiskey, and the talk of big money. How's a seven-year-old supposed to know that it's not Hollywood?

He insists. "All right," I say, "it's Hollywood. Where's your sister?"

While talking to him I have lost track of her. Sam and I run quickly through the set and the laundry room, through the empty sound stages and past the security guard, who has not seen her, to the pockmarked plain. I'm starting to panic.

Sam stays cool. He points. We run across the craters to Horse Heaven. He knows his sister. We find her in a motel room caressing a dark beauty who could be a stand-in for the Black Stallion if he wasn't too rich to work.

"Forget the hotel," Jessica says, "I want to stay here." She likes the granite pillars of the stable, the crystal chandeliers, the ever-present staff.

I tell her the truth. "We can't, it's too expensive."

She throws a pebble in disgust. Two Mexican gardeners run to pick it up. Another follows us with a vacuum-intake hose, sucking up the dust of our footsteps. These horses have all had their teeth capped, and several are in analysis.

"Who wants to hang around actors anyway," Jessica says, "and why is the director such a big shot? If he was smart he'd make a movie about horses."

"He has already made a movie about Billy the Kid," I tell her.

"He's got to do something new. Anyway, I don't tell him what to do. It's my job to watch, OK?"

I promise an evening trip to the hotel gift shop. Jessica reluctantly agrees to leave the stable.

When we return to the studio, the poker game has scattered and the picketer is back on the parking lot. The parking lot is big enough to land an airplane. It contains four maroon-and-gray rented Fords, a gray van, and the picketer. He has a gray beard and wears a cowboy hat. On that big lot against all that emptiness he looks like an extra in the cowboy version of *Gandhi*.

In the office the director is pronouncing it Gandy, like candy, to annoy the accountant, who has just returned from India. The accountant is almost as well groomed as the horses. He brings his laundry to the studio every day. He carries hangers full of pressed clothes over one shoulder and uses his other hand to make dramatic gestures about India. The director drinks his Scotch and laughs.

The primary actors are practicing being cool. They're all in their early twenties, two whites and two blacks. One of the blacks plays a killer. On the plane he scared the stewardesses out of their smiles. He wears clothes that someone else slept in. His fingers look like ice picks.

"C'mere, little girl," he says to Jessica. He's trying to be friendly but she runs downstairs to the sound stage. There it is quiet. The set looks like what it is, a big dollhouse. It's an army barracks with about a dozen beds, a small office at the rear, and a very white bathroom to one side.

Jessica lies down on one of the cots. She wants to forget the movie people and daydream about the horses across the prairie. She touches the bed to make sure it's real because she can see that the tan buildings outside the window only have fronts. The bed is real, the wool blanket even makes her skin itch. She pulls it back, lies down, and tries to fall asleep, but just when she gets comfortable she smells smoke.

It's the director. He's on his belly in front of the sergeant's cadre room lighting wadded-up balls of crinkly paper. He throws them in the air and then ducks as if they're grenades.

"I don't want to know when we first see this paper burning what the background is. When those things start going up you shouldn't know what they are and we're never going to explain."

Sam loves it. As he watches the director play, Sam suddenly understands what all this is about. He gets on his belly and crawls over to the director, who is lighting wad after wad of paper that his helpers keep handing to him. Sam is jealous. He is not allowed to play with matches and he knows it. He is also angry because he couldn't bring his friend, Richard. The director's friend, Bill, is upstairs drinking, and the producer's friend, Gene, is upstairs talking on the telephone. Sam wants a friend too. He understands that you need a friend when you spend so much time just waiting.

"Only the producers and directors get to bring their friends along," I tell Sam.

"Why?"

"The director because he's important, they couldn't do any of this without him. The producer because he's rich."

"Then I'll be a producer," Sam says, "and bring Richard next time. Producers probably don't have to be real rich."

As it turns out, Sam is right. But at least on the first day I think the producer is rich. Children know better. I rely on history; they use far more sophisticated diagnostic methods. On our first day in Las Colinas, Jessica and Sam administer a Rorschach test to the director. They present him with a choice of tattoos.

"I once tattooed dogs for a living," he tells Sam.

"Just select a tattoo," Sam says. "No verbal responses, please." The production crew gathers around to watch the director select a tattoo the way they came together within seconds to play poker while they stood around an empty desk. Bill, the director's buddy, tries to give the director a clue but the director waves him off.

The producer is disgusted. Left out of the circle, he watches from the background.

The choice of tattoos includes a pirate, a devil, a snake, a motorcycle, a dagger, a heart, a watermelon, and Annie.

The director chooses the pirate. Sam licks the tattoo and then presses it against the director's bicep. The test is over.

"Everyone knew he'd pick a pirate," I say to the producer. "It's the most obvious choice for this swashbuckling man."

"Of course," Bill says. "In Europe they think he's a pirate, a revolutionary. We just came back from showing *Elvis* in Cannes and Venice. In Europe he's a folk hero. They think he fights the establishment, they make it a lot more dramatic. You know the European film kids think all film is revolutionary. They think we are against the government."

"He would have chosen the devil," the producer says, "but he already has one." He points to one of the director's assistants. She sits on a chair beside the empty coat rack. She wears a black turtleneck sweater and black corduroy trousers. "She's the devil on the farm," the producer says. "She's alienated him from everyone. She's turning him against me."

The producer's grimness is enough to make you pack up your tattoos and head for the safety of the horses, but the young actors keep the room lively. Luke, one of the white actors, is fresh from an after-school special, *From Heaven with Love.* He is running around the office with his fingers around his eyes forming a Lone Ranger mask, describing how he chased down a bank robber on 59th Street.

"I'm probably a hero," he says.

The production manager is testing a walkie-talkie with an antenna above his ear.

"You now own six of these," he tells the director.

"Someday I'll be broke and come to you for help," the director says, "and you'll say, 'I'd like to do something for you but I have a family and I need all the interest I can earn on my money. But don't you still own six walkie-talkies with antennas?' "

The children and I are sitting on the floor near the coat rack reading a fund-raising flyer that the producer has prepared. It advertises a limited partnership for a cable TV and film production.

The producer comes to sit near us. He tells us he has been working on this project for six years. He's now thirty-three.

"I had to raise an extra hundred thousand to obtain the cable TV rights. I didn't have the money. My partner, Gene, washed dishes in Aspen to raise the money."

"How much do you need for this movie altogether?" Sam asks.

"One point four million," he says. "Just read the prospectus."

"I can't read big numbers yet," Sam says, but he calls Jessica and me aside. "If this guy's friend got a hundred thousand dollars washing dishes, why can't we raise the one point four million and become the producers?"

We approach the director.

He likes the idea. After all, if playwrights can take a hundred thousand from dishwashers, why can't directors get one point four million from kids? Anyway, the director has a deep grudge against children. He gave them an operatic, unsentimental mythical Sinbad smelling like the ocean and they preferred that candy-eating midget E.T.

We strike a deal and seal it with a dagger tattoo above the director's left nipple.

A Dallas business broker is eavesdropping. He has been listening to Bill tell about how he once got a train to begin moving away while Richard Nixon was giving a campaign speech, but the broker is not interested in Nixon. He is in the studio because he senses a lot of desperation about money. He wants a quick 10 percent finder's fee.

"These kids won't deliver," he tells the director. He is tall and smokes a cigar and has a three-inch scar down his left cheek.

"Where'd you get that cut?" Sam asks.

"I was scratched on the floor of the Commodities Exchange." He stares Sam down. "It could happen to you too. This is no business for a kid."

"Go tell it to Lucas and Spielberg," Sam says. "Kids have a wrap on this business. You might as well move up north and apply for unemployment. Who in his right mind would give an adult one point four million bucks?"

The broker calls me aside. "Listen," he says, "I tried to warn your kid to stay away. I take no further responsibility."

I would be a little intimidated if it were not for my nephew's recent experience. My nephew lives in Marin County, California. He had an orphan friend who wanted to finance his own Bar Mitzvah. To help raise money my nephew silk-screened some pornographic photos onto 100 percent cotton fitted sheets. He sold the sheets by direct mail. The concept escalated. He's sixteen now and has twenty-six employees. Twelve-year-olds from all over the country are raising funds for spectacular Bar Mitzvahs by peddling these sheets in their very straight suburban neighborhoods. My nephew is going right from high school into Stanford's MBA program. "When you have computer literacy," my nephew told us, "you leave the mob in the nineteenth century."

"The kids have the future in their bones," I tell the broker.

"It's on your head," he says. As he goes across the office toward the director he kicks over the pile of limited partnership brochures that Jessica and Sam have formed into a two-story house of cards.

"Don't monkey with the small fry," the broker says. "I've got a real estate investor, also reasonably young, thirty maybe, who is giving his wife a million dollars. She wants to go into the entertainment business."

"Bring her around," the director says. He pours himself another drink.

"Does that mean our deal is off?" Sam asks.

"Money talks," the director says, "and this is not a silent picture."

While Sam, Jessica, and I go back to Houston to see if we can raise the money, the broker tries to arrange a meeting between the director and the Dallas couple with the million. The producer is suddenly out of the picture.

The director tells the producer and his buddy to leave the hotel and get a lawyer, because he has not produced a single dollar and everyone is tired of waiting. The director takes away the producer's rented car, leaving the parking lot even emptier.

The producer moves to a much more expensive hotel and gets a better rental car. He doesn't need to get a lawyer; he already has four.

"I wanted to watch the film being made," he says. "Instead I have to spend all my time negotiating with lawyers. That's the one thing I'm really good at."

The director's lawyer flies in from New York and the studio owner's lawyer drives in from downtown Dallas to settle things with the Teamsters. The Teamsters are easiest to please. All they want is a job for the lone picketer. When it is arranged, he finds himself a good spot in the office next to the director's buddy. The teamster is immediately friendly. He introduces himself as the "dumb-ass who's going to drive the film to the airport." He talks nonstop movie industry gossip at a slow steady pace like cable TV news.

The director's lawyer and the producer's lawyer engage one another at the First City Bank Building. The director has a little money; the producer has none. While the lawyers go at it downtown, the broker brings the millionaire couple to the studio to see some of the film. The husband is excited about giving his wife the million. They both love the brand-new clean studio and enjoy the catered vegetarian lunch. When they see some of the dailies they are not sure they want to put their million into entertainment.

"It's not your average Saturday night date movie," the director's assistant says.

In Houston, Sam is having the same problem raising funds that the producer encountered in Hollywood and in Dallas. The director's name means nothing to the kids. They want a star. If there's a role for a black they insist on Gary Coleman. If there are soldiers they want war, and if there's war they want total annihilation. They also want motorcycles and karate.

The kids are not impressed by any of the director's old movies except *Paul's Coop.* They like that one because it is about birdshit.

Richard, Sam's friend, advises Sam to invest in film indirectly. "You want Columbia Pictures," Richard says, "then you buy Coca-Cola stock. You want Paramount, you buy Gulf and Western. You don't take direct risks on a crazy old man in Dallas."

Sam reminds Richard that if they buy corporate stock they won't be able to return to Dallas and crawl around on the floor and play with the director. This causes Richard to change his mind. Together he and Sam organize and lobby the student council representatives of all the junior high schools in Houston.

"Those student council guys are mostly girls," Richard says, "but they control all the candy and cookie and gym bag and car wash money that is collected to send the ninth graders on a school trip to

Washington, D.C. They're holding a junior high pension fund,'' Richard says. "There's only a few homeroom advisers between us and very big money. And nobody knows less about cash flow than homeroom teachers.''

When Sam phones him with the conditions, the director refuses Gary Coleman. He wants no further casting advice. "I had plenty from the first producer.''

He reads Sam a few excerpts from the producer's memo on casting.

> "The kids must be nineteen, twenty, twenty-one, or twenty-two, unsullied and undefiled performers, zesty and scrubbed hard. Travolta, Hutton, O'Keefe, and Carradine et al. are out, and I think none—with the plain exception of Travolta, of course, whose Billy (actually, the anchor to the piece) still beguiles the hell out of me—is an attraction by himself capable of conferring further desirability to our prospective licensees, anyway.
>
> "I believe the spot for hot casting is Sergeant Kelly. . . . Some proposals for casting as Kelly:
>
> "Carroll O'Connor (can we absorb Archie Bunker?).
>
> "Marlon Brando (too fat and too old?).
>
> "Gene Hackman (low profile, but can't Hackman incomprehensibly transfigure the commonplace?).
>
> "Robert Mitchum (if he wouldn't be so damned conscientious; can Mitchum act with his whole body and have a frisky, high time?).
>
> "Dick Van Dyke, on the mark with 'hair whitish and cut short,' a Goofy-Kelly to somebody's Pluto-Campbell, or maybe Van Dyke's a better Campbell opposite O'Connor's Kelly (don't you believe Carroll and Dick'd actually play 'hide-and-seek'?)."

"It's this cast, this script, this set, or nothing at all. I can raise the money myself if I have to.''

While Sam thinks over the ultimatum and promises to get together with the junior high board, the director uses his last cash to buy out the producer's screen and cable TV rights. It's the first time he has ever solely financed a film.

The director is talking tough to Sam but he is in deep trouble. His Malibu house, his last big asset, is now only three and one half inches from the Pacific Ocean. His wife and sons have flown back to sandbag the area and evict the present tenants, who are in the midst of an end-of-the-world party.

The director and Bill pace the office trying to decide whom they can still count on to raise a little production money.

"It's too bad the Shah is gone," Bill says. "The Shah was always a possibility." They drink to the end of the Shah.

"Nobody in Hollywood will give me a nickel," the director says. "They think I'm mean and ornery. In Dallas all they understand is real estate. If I needed twenty times as much to build an apartment complex with its own theater I'd have the money overnight. We could budget the film out of incidentals, a promotional expense."

"It's not a bad idea," Bill says, "but can we stay sober enough to talk to carpenters?"

"I'm not good at real life," the director says.

The teamster joins them. "Liza Minnelli was in town last night, appearing at a dinner theater. She wowed two SRO audiences. The menu included veal cutlets in white sauce, asparagus tips, and chili."

"You know," Bill says, "Qaddafi might be a possibility. He has been lying low since Billy Carter."

"Do you know him?" the director asks.

"No," Bill says, "but dictators are all alike."

"Jack Elam," the teamster says, "likes a little tomato juice mixed in his beer, and Jack Nicholson will never use a straw. Joan Didion was in town last night. I drove her to the airport. She didn't have time to stop over here."

"What the hell," the director says, "let's call Qaddafi." They walk over to the secretary.

"How do you call Libya?" they ask her.

"You can direct-dial Tripoli," she says. "My second husband worked there for three months. Lots of Texans do business in Libya."

"Call collect," the teamster says. "I heard Brando tell Fonda that Qaddafi accepts all collect calls."

The secretary places the collect call, but Qaddafi is in seclusion in the desert. He will not accept any calls until after Ramadan.

"Scratch him," the director says. "That leaves us with the kids in Houston."

"Call them back," Bill says, "and promise to use Gary Coleman. You can make up a gimmicky role for him, can't you? Maybe he can be a neighborhood shoeshine boy."

"There's no neighborhood. It's a barracks."

"So we'll shoot a neighborhood. Goddamn Dallas is full of neighborhoods."

"We could," the director says, "or Coleman could play one of the sergeants. We could say he's been wasted below the knees."

The director calls Sam to say Gary Coleman is OK but there is now a new condition. The junior high girls want Ricky Schroeder to play one of the white boys.

"Goddamn," the director says, "I've got to get out of this business." He hangs up.

Sam calls right back. "I don't like it either," he says, "but the purse strings here are controlled by sixth- and seventh-grade girls—they want Ricky. If you give us Gary and Ricky, I can have one point three million to you tomorrow. That's all there is in the D.C. trip fund. You'll have to get the last ten dimes elsewhere. Maybe try the mob for a short-term loan. We get half the net," Sam says, "and no more buttinsky from us. Once Gary and Ricky are in place, all decisions are yours."

They finalize the deal over the phone.

"There's one other thing," Sam says, "and this is just a suggestion, nothing binding: the junior high girls all think there ought to be a song, a kind of soft rock, and they can't believe you're going to do a movie without any girls. They want a girl too; they don't care who she is."

"That's no problem," the director says. "The projectionist at the studio looks like Meryl Streep's double. I was thinking of using her anyway."

"When Meryl was here shooting *Silkwood,*" the teamster says, "she refused to walk near the barrels labeled DANGER—RADIOAC-

TIVE MATERIALS. She gets into her characters. She wanted a lead vest and protective mittens, and she is so fair that she needs sunburn lotion with a protective grading above eight."

The director's lawyer flies to Houston to brief the homeroom teachers. The producer's lawyer sues the director's lawyer for leaving the scene of litigation. The producer's friend returns to Aspen to wash dishes for the next investment opportunity. The director's friend flies to California to be quizzed by F. Lee Bailey on *Lie Detector* about his relations with Richard Nixon. The director's family is still in Malibu piling sandbags against the raging Pacific. The horses are all looking out of their picture windows, hoping to be cast as extras.

The junior high students in Houston add pornographic sheets to their sales list and pack their bags for D.C.

The director is on the floor. He's playing with fire and he loves it.

Stranger at the Table

I write from weariness. I am tired of explaining the difference between meat and milk, a split hoof and an unsplit, a cow and a pig, a catfish and a red snapper.

You are hearing from a person who has never tasted a shrimp, a filet mignon, a ham sandwich, a pork chop, a lobster newburg, or even a plain old run-of-the-mill cheeseburger. The Whopper is a stranger to my lips, so too the Big Mac, the Dude, and old Jack-in-the-Box. It's even hard to find a graham cracker made with vegetable shortening, and a marshmallow is something I taste once a year when it arrives from New York for Passover held together by algae gelatin, all stiff and smelling of the sea.

I memorize the ingredients listed on the sides of packaged foods and search the surface for arcane markings known only to the initiated. A Ⓤ or a K makes my heart leap; the word "pareve" is like a personal call at a pay phone.

I am the minority of the minority, the dinner guest you can never satisfy. When I ask "What's cooking?" I expect an answer.

I used to think that in New York I might wander the streets smacking my lips like a freed slave hardly knowing what to desire next. There, I thought, every day must be a Christmas morning, bagels growing in trees, a trellis of kreplach, foot-long kosher hot dogs, unlarded gingerbread men dancing in the street, Ronald McDonald singing about a "Big Irving," the Kentucky Colonel in a Yiddish accent praising boiled chicken.

Alas, in my three trips to Manhattan I've had as much trouble finding something I could eat as I do in Houston. In some ways it's worse. There, I've made the mistake of asking if it's kosher. I've asked full of hope, admittedly innocent and naive. The waiter glares at me as if I'm an Arab terrorist. He mumbles about somewhere in Brooklyn or the Bronx, then stands over me like an executioner. The five-page menu lies before me like a harem. The executioner picks up his pen, and though I know there must be a lot I could try, the waiter refuses to help. I quickly retreat to the safety of egg salad.

To comfort me at a time like this I recall the unknown waitress of my youth. She epitomizes the many strangers I am grateful to, but she is specific, a middle-aged woman in a lonely delicatessen in Detroit; she came to my aid when I needed her most. I was about ten years old. My father was taking me to my first big-league baseball game, a doubleheader between the Detroit Tigers and the Boston Red Sox.

It was a five-hour drive to Detroit. I was too excited to sleep the night before. For breakfast I had only thin cocoa. I carried my glove hoping for a foul ball and my Scripto pencil for autographs just in case I ran into Al Kaline or Ted Williams in the parking lot. At some rest stop in central Michigan I left my lunch on a picnic bench. I wanted to go to my first big-league game without the burden of a half-pound tuna sandwich on yellow challah. I wanted my hands free for pop fouls, in my lap I wanted only a scorecard. In love with my heroes, I discounted hunger.

By the time we got to the ball park it was the fast of Yom Kippur in the back seat. My father circled Briggs Stadium looking for a parking place. "There it is," he said. Weak and dizzy, I arose to see that gorgeous dark green stadium surrounded by a rotting ghetto. A row of solemn black men held placards stating *Parking $1.00* and pointed to their backyards. They were like pagan priests before the big round mosque of baseball.

My stomach roared. My fingers were hardly strong enough to unlock the door. "You've got to eat something," my father said. He turned away from the stadium toward a bleak business district.

There in a restaurant where there seemed nothing I could eat I met her. My father didn't know what to do with me. I was so hungry that I left my baseball glove in the car. The waiter told me that the hot dogs were kosher, but I also noticed every variety of swine on his menu.

I ordered a Coke. My father, almost in tears, begged me to eat so I could enjoy the game.

"Tell him to eat, please," he asked the waiter.

The waiter gave me a "Let the little bastard starve" look and returned to the kitchen.

Then she came through the swinging varnished doors, this genuinely decent woman.

"Honey," she said, "come with me."

She pulled my head off the counter and took me into the kitchen. She let me watch while she put two kosher hot dogs into a thick plastic bag and then boiled them in the bag.

She produced a packaged rye bread and pointed out the vegetable shortening. What I remember most is her dishwasher. I was so hungry that I would have eaten kosher food from the floor but she gave me a lecture on water temperature, convincing me that her plates were more thoroughly boiled than sinners in hellfire. She brought out a side dish of vegetarian baked beans and sat next to me while I ate. She even gave me some hard candy for dessert.

The Tigers lost both games; I caught no foul balls. I've forgotten everything that happened at that astonishing dreamlike ball park, but the interlude in the dingy restaurant and the kindness of that anonymous waitress still fortify me against some of the despair that goes along with being the stranger at the table.

Most of my hunger took place less dramatically, at places like the A&W where my high school friends congregated. The Calvinists complained that they couldn't go to school dances; the Catholics were giving up asparagus for Lent. Cheeseburgers and chili dogs gave them the strength to continue their laments.

I told them they were amateurs at denial.

"What you do doesn't even count," one of my friends said. "It's too crazy to figure out."

He was right. I don't even know how to begin to explain. It has taken a few thousand years to make up these kosher rules. I only want to tell you what it feels like.

It is the heart and soul of being an outsider, the schizophrenia of social life. Eating has always been almost as much a social as a biological event. When the angels came to Abraham he slaughtered a kid to make them dinner. For all we know he seethed that kid in its mother's milk; there were no rules then. Abraham, busy escaping Sodom and establishing a multitude, didn't worry about *kashrut,* but he did know that when someone came to visit, you washed his feet and then invited him to dinner. Imagine it, divine beings, bearers of the celestial message, their feet have touched the stones of heaven, they have not been hungry for centuries, but just to be decent they sit with the patriarch.

Of course, the pagan gods were always feasting and drinking, and why not? Even mythological people understand a good time.

Your hunger satisfied in the company of one to seven others, the conversation, the drinks, the anticipation before and the sleepy fullness after: the meal in all its parts is the perfect recipe for averting melancholy. In it mankind turns necessity into high civility.

It seems so easy now that we don't have to hunt and kill or even cook if we don't want to, so easy to walk into a restaurant and order. But try it this way: "Excuse me, waiter, do you have a kosher table? I mean do you separate your milk and meat products, do you stay away from pork and shellfish, are your animals ritually slaughtered, is the meat then salted and soaked, the entrails inspected for irregularities? Do you keep extra sets of crockery for Passover, is challah 'taken,' and is there a constant watchman familiar with all the rules? If not, I guess I'll pass and go to New York or Israel for lunch."

But if there is fish on the menu it can save a lot of carfare. Good old proletarian fish, nothing fancy, just gills and scales—tuna, salmon, trout, flounder, even a sardine in a pinch. The fish and the egg are the two animal proteins that are classified "pareve," neither milk nor meat. Forever in limbo, the fish and the egg sustain public dining for the kosher few.

It's only flesh that demands vigilance; the vegetable kingdom is entirely kosher. We can eat the bruised fruit, the thistly artichoke, the indeterminate tomato. We freely mix rice and beans, peas and carrots, bananas and peaches; if we wanted to we could even floss our teeth with blades of grass or chew on bark. Dandelions are kosher, figs, mushrooms, literally everything that grows—from the shy potato to the symbolic apple. The Yiddish language, created during the eight hundred years in which the European Jews were locked into villages, their claustrophobic ghettos and villages, has few words for the grandeur of nature, but we're perfectly free to eat it all.

I hope that you are relieved to know that I am not starving. I can eat the rain forest and the tundra or be satisfied by a fruit salad.

Yet the world doesn't know much about what kosher means and it's partly the fault of those of us who are kosher and keep quiet about it. I've done it too, pretended lack of hunger, feigned a toothache, vegetarianism, change of life, anything to avoid explaining one more time to a well-intentioned gentile why I can't share a chicken-fried steak. We smile tight smiles, drink a lot of water, and are embarrassed by this little habit which we haven't managed to break in about two thousand years.

If you've ever known anyone kosher you might have been confused in a variety of ways. The law is the law but the interpretations are many. The absolutely orthodox will not eat anything in a non-kosher home or a public place. Their lips are sealed. But chances are you've hardly ever encountered such a person.

A far more prevalent type is the only-at-home kosher. This is an attempt by some Jews to hang onto the old culture without getting in the way of contemporary life. These people keep their home kosher but drop all prohibitions once they leave its threshold. It is as if they've discovered a special footnote, a Talmudic homeowners' policy. Since they do partake outside the home, kosher becomes a cultural symbol rather than a taboo, something you choose rather than an obligation.

Then there is the "everything but" way of kosher. This hearty appetite has gone almost all the way: a hamburger washed down with milk, squid, octopus, steak tartare—nothing stops him until he meets the pork chop. That crinkly innocuous piece of sinew recalls to him the ancient taboo. It's as if Moses himself arises from the plate to wave the finger of shame. Pork is the tough one, the hard core, the one animal absolutely prohibited when the Bible named names. The Jew who faces this one down may be beyond the hope of chicken soup. Most of the Jews I know will eat ham or bacon readily. These foods are so common that their origin in the flesh is overshadowed by familiarity. But mention a pork cutlet, a chop, a cold pork sandwich, pickled pig's feet, or even fried pork skins, and some Jews with the most liberated appetites will shudder like their great-grandparents huddled in the ghetto.

I don't know what statistical proportion of Jews makes any attempt to follow kosher laws. In Houston there are only two kosher butcher shops, and neither does a thriving business. The only kosher restaurant is the snack bar at the Jewish Community Center.

Most non-Jews who think they've eaten in a kosher restaurant have actually been in a "kosher style" delicatessen. These places, while they may satisfy the non-kosher, are actually a tease and an annoyance to the observant. They sometimes have kosher corned beef or salami, but they cut the meat alongside cheese, cook it with bacon, and consider kosher merely a culinary word like "French" or "home style."

This watered-down version is what most non-Jews and a considerable percentage of Jews probably mean by kosher: a kind of sandwich, a type of pickle, something highly spiced, exotic, in a general way "foreign." But there are such phenomena as kosher cheese, a kosher cookie, kosher bread; all these everyday non-meat foods are just as subject to the rules as the meat. If the corned beef is kosher but the bread is baked with animal shortening, you don't have a kosher sandwich. This may not disturb many people, but it suggests that the watchfulness of kosher eaters does not stop with the main course.

My major complaints are against those who violate salads. At a buffet I approach a green salad as confidently as Robert Redford at a singles bar. I grab the big tongs and start to load up. I see tomato, two kinds of lettuce, cucumber, radish, and then, peeking out from behind a big romaine leaf, a little cube of ham. Some clever chef has just wanted to make sure I get my daily portion of protein.

Just don't eat the ham, you're probably thinking, but here's the rub: the whole thing is now ruined for me. That tiny piece of ham might as well have been a quorum of roaches. I know that there will be other pieces, and anything in contact with that ham is not kosher. The entire salad bowl, even my plate, already half loaded with what I thought would be my main course, is now a total loss. I dump the salad into the bowl, go back to the top of the line for a new plate, and this time will watch out for the pieces of meat in the cold cream peas I am about to try. Full of hope, I see what looks like tuna salad. I get close, sniffing like a cat, but I can't tell. People in the line are starting to wonder about me. I ask the person behind me to smell it; he usually refuses. Then I seek out a busboy to ask if it's tuna or chicken salad.

"I'd like to know," I say. "It's important to me." I try to stay calm, patient. "Would you please find out?"

He'll usually go to the kitchen and come back ten minutes later. By then the people I'm with have already forgotten my name. I'm like someone who has died at sea and been thrown overboard.

"Chicken," he says, smiling, thinking he's done me a big favor.

I approach a colorful dessert combination—yellow, orange, and white. I suspect marshmallow but am hoping coconut. It's marshmallow, the consistency maintained by gelatin, the confectioners' glue made of boiled animal hooves. So much for my lunch. I settle for a hard-boiled egg and a Coke, but by now I feel too betrayed to eat.

An excellent rule for dealing with even suspected kosher guests (also vegetarians): Unmeat your salads, no pink in the green. It's also not a bad idea to put out something that's easily identifiable: an apple, a banana, a carrot. I don't have to ask anyone to smell a carrot, and such a simple thing is almost always a greater delight to me than my host realizes.

Kosher, you see, is not a style. It is an ancient, powerful, unyielding code. It is a way of ordering the world, an unconscious systematic recognition of the price we pay to eat flesh. It begins in the biblical prohibition against seething a kid in its mother's milk and is reinforced by the taboo against eating the living being or drinking blood.

Presumably the hearty Chaldeans and the populace of Nineveh and Babylon didn't always bother with niceties like the actual death of the animal they were eating. To them fast food was genuinely that. The step back from this raw pleasure is surely the origin of the kosher prohibitions. In dim antiquity it signals a kind of revolutionary turn from cannibalism and human sacrifice to the more subdued atmosphere of animal sacrifice and food taboos.

But nobody is kosher for such anthropological reasons, and only a zealot comes to it late in life. For most of us, kosher is a translation of childhood love into food. One of the duties of my childhood was helping out in this altogether careful business of watching what you eat.

It wasn't only kosher, sometimes it was just safety. I watched my grandfather as he ate a fishhead every Friday night. My job was to feed him bread when he choked on the small bones and to call for help if tears came to his eyes. I looked at the fish's dead eyes and at my grandfather's false teeth resting in the china closet. When necessary, I pounded his back and pulled on his earlobes. I did my job.

For my grandmother I checked to make sure the pilot was lit in the gas stove. For everyone in the household I interpreted the chemical additives of food. By the age of eight I was a little Ralph Nader on preservatives.

I know that I could eat a cold pork sandwich in a synagogue on Yom Kippur and live happily ever after. I know that pork and shellfish are probably no less clean and no less well prepared than beef or chicken. I know that the rules make no sense in our "modern age," and as you can see I recognize that it's often a pain in the neck to find something to eat and even more of a pain trying once again to explain to others what I won't eat and why.

I do it in spite of all the difficulties, simply because it seems right. I don't feel superior to Jews who have given it up, nor do I envy them or the gentiles who eat what they choose. I'm fascinated by the liberty to taste at will, but it seems no more available to me than the wealth of Saudi Arabia.

One of the sublime biblical lines is God's definition of himself: "I am what I am." So are we all.

Whatever its origins, I am the offspring of generations of the kosher. One of my great-great-grandmothers, when she came to America, suspected all canned foods. My great-grandparents preferred the poverty and anti-Semitism of Russia to the riskiness of remaining observant Jews in the new world. My little grandmother, seasick all the way from Poland in the third class of a rotting ship, listened to her pots and pans clatter beside her as she sucked on a lemon. She carried her crockery across the Atlantic because she didn't know if she could find kosher pots in America.

My breast milk was kosher, my baby food; I learned the difference between meat and milk long before I knew the difference between boys and girls. A hamburger with a glass of milk is as unlikely to me as rooting for the Yankees, a ham sandwich as unappealing as a computer printout.

The prohibitions, rooted in food, become embodied in esthetics and ethics as well. I know how limited my foods are, but I don't miss what I don't desire.

If I wanted to taste the forbidden I would break the taboos. Yet what I might eat seems such a small pleasure to gain compared to the satisfaction of pleasing my ancestors, the dead as well as the living.

Most Americans don't consciously think that much about their ancestry, as if we were all on the *Mayflower* and at Gettysburg. "Land where my fathers died, land of the pilgrims' pride" isn't historically accurate. My "fathers" died in Russia, Poland, Lithuania, Galicia, Germany, Serbia. They lived their long and hard lives imagining

Jerusalem and watching what they ate. The DNA of their genes is mine, also the scope of their diet.

I can put up with the awkwardness of what I'll eat because it has never spread to what I can think. There are no non-kosher thoughts or ideas.

I remember once telling a rabbi at a teenage youth meeting that I saw no particular reason why the world couldn't get along very well without Jews. He was eating a peach at the time, sucking the pit. He almost choked. He called in my grandfather. I must have sounded to him like a neo-Nazi. But that was his problem. Thinking is all kosher, and I sometimes wonder if drawing the line in one realm doesn't give me greater freedom in others. Maybe that's a fantasy; still, the line is there.

"Show me where to stand," Archimedes said, "and I'll move the world." "Show me where to sit," I say, "and maybe there'll be something I can eat." If I have to move the world, I'll do it with vegetable shortening.

Carbo-Loading

M y first significant carbohydrates came from beer. Mom was a miler, but to nurture embryonic me she didn't even walk stairs. She spent eight hours a day in bed. While nursing she developed a taste for beer. Vaguely, I recall foam at the nipple. Dad sat beside us and sipped from long-necked bottles.

He'll be a hurdler, they thought, judging by my stride. As they cuddled me they stretched my tendons from the ankle to the knee. Dad wanted a sprinter, Mom hoped for distance. When I was thirty she got her way.

By then I had been a beer man for a decade. When I finally started to run I felt like a washing machine. The beer swirled within amid the colorful jungle of entrails. I had no stamina for a final sprint, no burst of glucose for the hills. I was always on rinse and hold.

My doctor said that because of my drinking I had developed little pockets of beer, not just the well-known belly but beer bulge at the wrists, behind the ears, between the vertebrae. As I ran, these bits of beer quivered like dangling earrings.

Dr. Isle is a runner too. He figures that if it increases his working life by just four years it will make him $1 million richer. So he cut the million from life insurance and added it to malpractice. He runs fifteen miles a day. Lots of times he's too mellow to diagnose. Tumors and arrhythmias float by as unnoticed as dull movies, but he perks up for a stretched Achilles tendon or a swollen knee joint.

After he drains my pouches with a long needle, Isle looks me in the eye. "Cut the beer," he says, "if you ever want to run a three-hour marathon."

Sweet Nurse Phillips bends to lace my Nikes. I hobble into the waiting room and crush my last six-pack in the wastebasket.

"Good for you," Nurse Phillips says. There are bright tears in her eyes. The patients cheer.

For the next two weeks I take Gatorade injections and run on a treadmill beside my bed. Then during my first outdoor ten miles my hair turns the color of autumn, my legs cramp, and my ankles crackle like chestnuts.

"Carbohydrate depletion," Dr. Isle says. He gets me into reclining position on the examining table. Nurse Phillips spoons dry Cheerios through my wind-chapped lips.

"Ten thousand cc's," he orders.

Her tender feeding revives me. The Cheerios that fall to my legs she spears on the point of a long fingernail. She does an impromptu cardiogram by putting her ear to nine different spots on my chest. Her tight curls tickle. When she embraces me, I respond.

"It's normal," she says.

Isle prescribes a box of unsweetened cereal for dessert every day. "Load up on carbohydrates," he says. "Protein will never get you more than ten miles. Amino acids are selfish. They want to stay the way they are. That's why I don't believe in life on other planets. Protein is insular and xenophobic. It's all left-handed. It's expensive and hard to maintain. I hate it as much as sugar, but what can you do? It's all there is. After twenty miles the body eats itself."

Nurse Phillips hands me a plastic packet with professional samples of bee pollen, desiccated liver, and body punch. I ask her to go out with me on Saturday night.

"The Boston Marathon is in two months," she says. "I'll be doing stretching exercises every spare minute until then."

"I'll see you in Boston," I say, "at the finish line." We make a date for the twenty-seventh mile.

"I hope you'll really be there," she says. "I hope you've got what it takes."

"I'll be there," I say. I pat the top of her nurse's cap.

What it takes, I learn, is more than what you have. I learn this from all the experts. The books confirm what Isle says. He has not deluded me. Carbo-loading will only get you twenty miles. For the last six you eat your heart out. In my training, even with Gatorade and bee pollen and seventy-dollar heel inserts, I can't make it past twenty miles.

I think of Nurse Phillips in Boston, moist and anxious at the finish, seeking me. Still I can't get past twenty. I think of Jesus on the cross, martyrs on the rack, witches at the stake, but my own misery is not diminished by the suffering of others.

In desperation I bone up on personal cannibalism. The prime minister of India drank his own urine, various women have sampled their breast milk, and all of us suck blood from our snakebites and swallow great quantities of phlegm and saliva. But none of this historicism helps.

Finally, on the advice of an experienced marathoner, I check into a running clinic. There I am immediately weighed naked under water and am relieved to learn that only 9 percent of my person is fat. This is better than average, so I have no excuse there. Furthermore, my resting pulse is forty and I can hit alpha waves at the mere mention of the word *peace* in any language.

I am a difficult case. The director assigns me to a running therapist. "Pick your speed," the therapist says, "stay comfortable, and don't try to impress me. You will for a while in middle distance try to model yourself after me. There may even be a passing boyish crush, a temporary identity crisis. Don't worry. By fifteen miles or so it will be over. You will learn to identify a stride and a gasping pattern that is totally unique."

The therapist has a gray beard, as I expected, and wears conservative dark gray shorts. He takes notes on a dictaphone no larger than a digital stopwatch.

My parents and childhood take the first five miles. We hit puberty at about thirteen. I talk on the exhale. Every three miles we take a two-minute break from analysis. During the rest I jog in silence. He encourages me to have pastoral fantasies during those intervals. "Pretend you are a gazelle," he says, "a gazelle along the verdant banks of the ancient Tiber, or a sleek antelope galloping toward some lush African watering place."

He is right. I do admire his long authoritative stride. I am enthralled by the way he hears me out, knowing exactly when to press the dictaphone. To him my lack of endurance is just a job. When I am finished he'll shower and take on someone else. What strength he has, what dedication. He reads the admiration of my silence.

"Look," he says, "body language aside, I don't think this should be a block for you. Let's just go on. By sixteen or seventeen miles it should be over. Believe me, it's just sort of Oedipal."

I get nostalgic then about my early training, my blue Adidas Dragons, the high school track, my first seven-minute mile.

"Speaking of time," he says, "you're doing an eight-fourteen pace and we're at the nineteenth mile." I know that he will stop at twenty. "The last six you're on your own. Even in therapy," he says, "I can't take you all the way. But I think you're ready."

At twenty miles an orderly in a golf cart is awaiting him. The orderly pours a bucket of water on my head, gives me a cup of Gatorade, and takes my therapist back to the clinic. "Good luck!" they shout.

I am in the deep woods now and it is almost dusk. Certain primal fears try to grip me, but my heart is too busy for fear. Twenty-one passes. This is all new territory. It's like suddenly growing four or five inches and having to relearn old habits like the length of a step. In my pride at having passed twenty-one miles I stumble on a tiny tree root. My ankle hurts. I'm unable to walk. When I'm not at the clinic as expected, the therapist himself comes out for me in the golf cart. He loads me onto the seat. "Nothing seems to be broken," he says, squeezing my right tibia and ankle. "There are obstacles in everyone's path. You'll have to be more wary in the future, but I think you'll make it."

And that, my friends, is as close as I came to 26 miles 385 yards until the day in Boston. Yes, I ran slow tens and twelves. I did sprints and fartleks. I ran hills and trained my breath on the steps of the football stadium. People who knew me in the beer days, even in the three-to-five-mile stage, were in awe of my leanness. At the track I lapped those who used to be my peers.

In Boston it's true I was alone and far from home. I had a bad night in a lumpy motel room. I was stiff and eager and maybe slightly overtrained. But I had eaten for the race. It was Monday. From the previous Sunday through Wednesday I had nothing but protein, meat at all three meals. At McDonald's I threw away the bun and held the double-beef patty and melted cheese in my bare hands. Instead of Coke I carried my own powdered beef broth, which I mixed with boiling water. Then from Thursday through Sunday I loaded carbos. With Dr. Isle's permission, of course, I had a six-pack on Sunday night. "Lots of carbos," he said, "and it will clean you out before the race." I ate miles of spaghetti and bought bread by the pound.

On Monday morning at the Hopkinton starting line I was ready. The stars of the distance world were all there pretending it was just another day. Frank Shorter ate a Ding-Dong and a banana, Bill Rodgers munched on gingerbread. Way up front, in the under-three-hour grouping, I thought I spotted Dr. Isle but I couldn't reach him in the throng. The one I really looked for, Nurse Phillips, was somewhere in the herd of four-hour women stretching their backs against trees, adjusting straps, fine-tuning themselves.

Well, I thought, I'll give it all I've got. Those were my big words to myself at the start. I said them over and over for the first four miles. I studied faces as they passed, then switched to subjects. I did philosophy from mile five to eleven, trying to form one discriminating sentence about Socrates, Kant, Spinoza, Kierkegaard, whomever. When I came to the authors of *How to Be Your Own Best Friend,* I knew my mind was wandering and let go of systematizing. I listened to the rhythm of my breath, which was unsteady as early as twelve miles into the race.

By fifteen miles, lots of women were passing me and I understood that I might not make it. Without despair I continued step by step.

If not for the nurse's cap I might not have recognized Miss Phillips as she pulled alongside. Her stride was lively. The insides of her thighs puckered. "Take one of these," she said, slipping me a brown tablet. "Dolomite."

I hesitated.

"It's just magnesium and calcium. It will help with the cramps." Though I could barely talk, esprit de corps was in my eyes. She ran alongside me, my inspiration and my pacer, until I ran out of myself. She says it was after twenty-four miles. My feet just stopped taking orders.

In the sudden stillness I thought someone had put me into the sidecar of a motorcycle. I heard the static of a CB radio. Eight or ten horsepower seemed to be propelling me. It was Nurse Phillips. In charity she had entered my nervous system.

"Women have more stamina," she said. "I knew it before liberation."

I could feel that layer of feminine softness give of itself cell by cell. Her generosity moved my heart.

"Save something for later," I moaned, "for childbirth and famine."

She held my hand.

"I can't make it," I gasped.

"There's more to life than the marathon," she said. "There's the twenty-five kilometers, the hill climbs, the five-kilometer sprint, the half marathon."

"I'm too old," I said.

"There's the submasters and the masters. There's Golden Age jogging and, finally, trots in the sunset."

"Without you I couldn't make it," I said. "The therapist told me the last six miles had to be alone."

"There will still be loneliness," she said. "Swollen joints and arthritis, varicose veins, arguments over money."

The finish line was in sight—the Hancock Building, the great tower of insurance.

"For you," I said with my last breath. "I did it for you." At the finish line I collapsed in her arms. People all around were doing the same. It looked like World War I in underpants.

She doused me in Gatorade. "At any pace," she said, "there is infirmity and disease. Carbo-loading will never be enough."

We bronzed our shoes and toasted one another in Body Punch.

"When our electrolytes balance," she said, "we'll live happily ever after."

We showered and went into training.

The American Bakery

I grew up in the heyday of ventriloquism. The dummy Jerry Mahoney was everyone's sweetheart. You could hardly go a day without hearing a joke about buttoning your lip or having a wooden head.

On the playground of my elementary school I practiced with all my might. I kept my lips close to the chain-link fence so that if they moved I would know it by the cold steel against them. My friends were doing the same. Two decades early, our playground was a herald of transcendental meditation. We were six years old, saying "om" to the fence, each of us hoping for our own dummy, a dummy who would supply all the punch lines, leaving us forever free to roam the playground practicing voice control.

Finally I got my dummy. An elderly cousin, moved by the seriousness of my tight-lipped practice, sent me an expensive one, a three-foot-high Jerry Mahoney in a cowboy outfit and an embossed half-face smile. But by the time my Jerry arrived he was too late; ventriloquism had already faded. The contestants on *The Original Amateur Hour* went back to thigh slapping and whistling through combs. My schoolmates, too, abandoned loneliness against the fence for kickball and pulling girls' hair. My dummy languished then as my wok and my food processor do now.

It took another twenty years for me to cast my voice again, this time into stories rather than dummies. It's a weak analogy, I know, and yet fiction seems sometimes like my dummy, like that part of myself that should get all the best lines. I want to be the straight man so that the very difference between us will be a part of the tension that I crave in each sentence, in every utterance of those wooden lips redeemed from silence because I practiced.

Yet the voice from the silence, the otherness that fiction is, doesn't need any metaphoric explanations. It's true that I tried ventriloquism, but it was my fascination with the English language itself that made me a writer. Its coyness has carried me through many a plot, entertained me when nothing else could. If not for love of words, I couldn't have managed eighth grade sitting next to Wayne Bruining during lunch, listening to the details of his escapades as a hunter. These were not adventure stories of life in the wild; they were the drab minutiae of taxidermy. While I held an oily tuna sandwich, Wayne lectured on how to skin a squirrel. He brought pelts to school and supplied the entire class with rabbits' feet. As Wayne droned on, I wondered in all the words that were new to me if he hunted in fens, glades, moors, vales, and dales. Though his subject was gory, Wayne was a good teacher. I could probably skin a squirrel, based on my memory of his conversations. I imagine that Wayne is still at it somewhere deep in the Michigan woods, showing his own son how to position a dressed buck over the hood of the car and then wipe the knife clean on the outside of his trousers.

My grandmother had a word for Wayne and most of my other friends: *goyim.* It explained everything. The hunting, the hubcap stealing, the smoking, the fighting—all were universal gentile attributes. *Goy* was a flat, almost unemotional word, but it defined everything I was not. There was some difficulty. Grand Rapids, Michigan, in the 1950s was not an East European ghetto, although my grandma did her best to blur the distinctions. World War I and poverty had moved her from her Lithuanian village, but even forty years in the wilderness of America did not make her learn English. She chose, above all, to avoid the language of the goyim. I told her about Wayne and everything else in Yiddish, which was the natural language of talking. I remember being surprised in kindergarten that everything happened in English. To us, English was the official language, useful perhaps for legal documents and high school graduation speeches, but not for everyday life.

My grandmother and I were quite a pair in the supermarket. Proud that I could read, I read all pertinent labels to her in loud Yiddish. The two of us could spend a long time in aisle four at the A&P over the differences between tomato paste and tomato sauce, while all around us gentiles roamed, loading their carts with what we knew were slabs of pork and shotgun shells. We wondered at them, these folks who could eat whatever they wanted and kill their own chickens. My grandma never learned English or strayed very far from her house, but she did glean from the gentiles a lust for technology. Our big nineteenth-century kitchen, which was also my playroom and her salon, was loaded with the latest. Before anyone else, we had an oven with a see-through door, a rotisserie, a Formica-topped dinette, and a frost-free refrigerator. The technology, though clearly "goyish," was never tainted. Sometimes I would come into the kitchen to find my grandmother admiring the simplest object, a cast-aluminum frying pan or a Corning Ware baking dish. Our kitchen needed only a wood-burning stove to become the kitchen in every Russian novel, yet in that old-fashioned place all the wonders of modern America blossomed. My grandmother never trusted the gentiles, but because of the way she savored kitchen gadgets, I know that at some time, probably before I was born, she gave up her fear of pogroms and settled down to take in, through translation and bargains, the available pleasures.

While she daydreamed in Yiddish and Americanized her domain, my grandfather worked in the American Bakery, among ovens that could bake two hundred loaves at once. He wore a white shirt, white trousers, a white apron, and a white cap. His hair was white and fine-textured. Puffs of flour emanated from him as he walked toward me. The high baking tables, the smell of the bread, the flour floating like mist, gave the bakery a kind of angelic feeling. In the front, two clerks sold the bread and customers talked in plain English. In the back, where the dough was rising, my grandpa yelled in Yiddish and Polish, urging his fellow bakers always to hurry. He went to the bakery long before dawn and would sometimes work twenty-four nonstop hours. He was already in his seventies. Twenty-four hours he considered part time. He did not bake what you might think; the American Bakery was true to its name. My grandpa toiled over white bread, sticky air-filled white bread, and cookies shaped like Christmas trees, green at the edges, blood red in the middle. He baked cakes for Polish weddings and doughnuts by the millions. My grandmother preferred store-bought baked goods. Their ghetto curses and old-world superstitions interrupted *I Love Lucy* and *The $64,000 Question.* He wished upon her a great cholera, a boil in her entrails, a solipsism deeper than despair.

My mother spent her energy running the household. My father earned our living as a scrap dealer. His work meant driving long distances in order to buy, and then to load upon his short-wheel-base Dodge, tons of steel shavings, aluminum borings, defective machinery—anything that could eventually be melted back to a more pristine condition. I rode with him when he didn't have to go very far. I had a pair of leather mittens, my work gloves, which I wore as I strutted among the barrels of refuse at the back of factories. I touched the dirtied metals. I wanted to work as my father did, using his strength to roll the barrels from the loading dock to the truck. When he came home he washed his hands with Boraxo, then drank a double shot of Seagram's Seven from a long-stemmed shot glass. I imitated him with Coke or ginger ale. He alone knew what I wanted and loved. My grandfather wanted me to be a rabbinic scholar, my grandmother thought I should own at least two stores, my sisters and my mother groomed me for a career as a lawyer or "public speaker." My father knew that I wanted to play second base for the Tigers and have a level swing like Al Kaline. I probably love and write about sports so much as a way of remembering him. I carry baseball with me always the way he carried my mittens in the glove compartment of a half-dozen trucks to remind him of his little boy who grew up to study the secrets of literature but still does not forget to check the Tigers' box score every morning of the season. When I was not listening to the Tigers or playing baseball or basketball myself, I was reading. A tunnel under Bridge Street connected the Catholic school, next to the American Bakery, to the West Side branch of the public library. I don't know what use the Catholic school made of the tunnel, but it was my lifeline. I would have a snack at the bakery, then move through the tunnel to reappear seconds later in that palatial library. In the high-ceilinged reading room I sat at a mahogany table. Across the street, my grandpa in the heat of the ovens was yelling at Joe Post in Polish and at Philip Allen in Yiddish; here the librarians whispered in English and decorated me with ribbons like a war hero, just because I loved to read. The books all in order, the smiling ladies to approve me, the smooth tables, even the maps on the wall seemed perfect to me. The marble floors of that library were the stones of heaven, my Harvard and my Yale, my refuge in the English language. What I learned from those boys' books was indeed American Literature. Wayne Bruining skinning squirrels was too close, too ugly, too goyish. But in the aura of the reading room, *The Kid from Tomkinsville* and *Huckleberry Finn* were my true buddies. I wanted to bedeck them with ribbons the way the librarians decorated me or, better yet, take them through the tunnel for a quick doughnut at the bakery.

When I came home from the library I sometimes told my grandmother in Yiddish about the books. We wondered together about space travel and the speed of light and life on other planets. If there was life on other worlds, she thought it was only the souls of the dead. She urged me to read less and think about someday owning my own store.

I think it was in that library that I finally came to distinguish the separateness of the Yiddish and English languages. I could speak and think in both, but reading and writing was all English. I specialized in reading and writing as if to solidify once and for all the fact that the written language was mine.

My sisters found the language through speaking. They won "I Speak for Democracy" contests; they were the Yankees and Dodgers of debate tournaments. I could barely hit my weight in Little

League, but their speech trophies lined the windowsills like mold. They stood in front of our gilded dining room mirror, speaking earnestly and judging their looks at the same time. They used their arms to gesture, they quoted *Time* magazine, their bosoms heaved. My mother stopped her chores to swoon at her lovely daughters. My grandma thought their padded bras were a clever way to keep warm. Patrick Henry himself could not have outdone the rhetoric in our dining room.

My sisters wanted it for me too, that state championship in debate which seemed automatic just because we spoke English. I resisted the temptation as a few years later I resisted law school. I admired my sisters before the mirror and I, too, longed to understand *Time* magazine, but I didn't want to win anything with my words. I just wanted to play with them. I was already in love. Instead of debate, I took printing.

I, too, made words, but words laboriously made, words composed on a "stick," with "leads" and "slugs," words spelled out letter by letter with precise spacing—words that had to be read, not heard.

My hero was Ben Franklin. On his tombstone it said only: BEN FRANKLIN PRINTER.

"Did he make a living?" my grandmother wanted to know.

"He made the country. He and George Washington and Alexander Hamilton, they made the whole country."

"Go on," she said. "You believe everything they tell you in school."

I did believe everything I learned, but I listened to her too. Her stories were sometimes about the very things I studied. She had lived through the Russian Revolution. In a house in Odessa, a shoemaker's daughter, she waited out the war until she could join her baker husband, already sporting two-tone shoes and a gold watch on the shores of Lake Michigan.

She had no political ideology; the Czar and the Communists were equally barbarous in her eyes. Once, though, she did hide a young Jew pursued by the Czar's police. It was my favorite story. To me, that young Russian became Trotsky himself hiding for half an hour among my grandmother's wedding aprons, feather beds, long-sleeved dresses, and thick combs, the very objects I hid among in our Michigan attic.

She didn't care about Trotsky or Ben Franklin, only about her grandson, who she thought was making a mistake by becoming a scribe rather than a merchant. Only once, shortly before she died, did I convince my grandmother that being a scribe was not my intention. "I make things up, I don't just copy them."

"I've been doing that all my life," she told me. "Everyone can do that."

In a way she was right: making things up is not very difficult; the difficulty is getting the sentences to sound exactly right.

I would still prefer to be the ventriloquist—to let the words come from a smiling dummy across the room—but I'm not good enough at buttoning my lip. An awkward hesitant clumsy sentence emerges. I nurse it, love it in all its distress. I see in it the hope of an entire narrative, the suggestion of the fullness of time. I write a second sentence and then I cross out that first one as if it never existed. This infidelity is rhythm, voice, finally style itself. It is a truth more profound to me than meaning, which is always elusive and perhaps belongs more to the reader.

Jacob wrestled with angels and I with sentences. There's a big difference, I know. Still, to me they are angels, this crowd of syllables. My great-uncle who came from the Russian army in 1909 straight to the American West told me he never had to really learn English. "I knew Russian," he said. "English was just like it." He bought horses, cattle, land. He lived ninety years and when he died he left me his floor safe, which sits now, all 980 pounds, alongside me in the room where I write. My eight-year-old daughter knows the combination, but there is nothing inside.

I don't know if that's a trope too—that safe that comforts me almost as if there were a way to be safe. There is no safety—not for my uncle, not for my sentences so quickly guillotined, not for me either. Yet I wish for the security of exact words, the security I knew as a four-year-old reciting the Gettysburg Address at patriotic assemblies in the Turner School auditorium.

I learned the Gettysburg Address from a book of great American documents that my father found in the scrap. It was a true found poem; Lincoln's cadences thrilled me long before I knew what they meant. Abe Lincoln was as anonymous to me as that Russian hiding in my grandmother's boudoir, but I could say his words, say them in English, in American, and as I said them the principal wept and teachers listened in awe to such a little boy reciting those glorious words. My parents coached me in Yiddish as they taught me to say "Four score and seven years ago," but I know that they wanted me to be an American, to recite the Gettysburg Address to prove beyond a doubt that I was an insider to this new lingo, to prove that our whole family understood, through my words, that somehow we had arrived, feather beds and all, to live next door to squirrel skinners.

Perhaps my grandmother was right. A store or two, or even a law office, makes a lot more sense than a love affair with words. At least in a business your goods and services are all there, all out in the open, and most of the time you even see your customers. To confront them and know what you're selling—those are pleasures the writer rarely knows. Believe me, reader, I would like to know you. Most of the time I am just like you, curled up on the sofa hoping not to be distracted, ready to enter someone else's fabric of words just as you are now in mine.

Across the room from me, the safe is stuck half open. My son's tiny socks lie beside it, my daughter's lovely drawing of a horse, the sky, a cloud, and a flower. I wish I could tell you more, and I will perhaps in stories and novels: there I'll tell you more than I know. There I'll conjure lives far richer than mine, which is so pedestrian that it would make you seem heroic were you here beside me. Take comfort, though, in these sentences. They came all the way from Odessa at the very least and have been waiting a long time. To you they're entertainment; to me, breath.

Pizza Time

Directions: You are a parent. Your mission is to raise your two children to become reasonably sane, decent, compassionate, capable adults. You must overcome all the obstacles on the board.

Enter Max, the father, pizza sauce from yesterday still on his whiskers.

Enter Jessica, nine, a cross between Annie and Ms. Pac-Man.

Enter Sam, six, in heat: "I love Chuck E. Cheese, I want to marry him."

Enter the chaperoned Cub Scouts ahead of us and a Little League team behind.

Enter Brad, Sam's friend.

Come in, children, parents, aficionados of the new technology. Come into the Pizza Time Theatre.

We enter a Pizza Time about twenty miles from downtown Houston. The subdivisions here are as entrenched as·superstitions, even though everything is brand new. Pizza Time is surrounded by unfinished mall space hungry for dry cleaners and liquor stores. When I enter I stand in amazement, bewildered as if I'm about to be X-rayed and await a technician's help. The children are right at home. Jasper Jowls tells jokes to Pasquale. The computerized flags salute us as we pass.

Jessica takes her tokens and heads toward Ms. Pac-Man. Sam trades dollars for tokens and goes to the far end of the game room to play Skee-ball. I walk through the pizza line, the salad line, the sundae line, and the fantasy forest. At Jasper's General Store I turn right into a cozy piano bar that is being vacated by Brownies.

In this more subdued atmosphere I think about the days when figuring your way out of a maze on a paper place mat used to be what you did while you waited for a pizza. I can even remember when there was no pizza.

"My love does it good to me" arises melodically from the orange-haired hippopotamus who works the piano bar. Her name is Dolly Dimples. Someone has pumped a quarter into her.

From my good seat close to the bosom of Dolly I can read some of the machines.

Directions: Blast alien ships . . .
Directions: Shoot the approaching enemy and enemy charges
. . .
Directions: Destroy monsters by blowing them up or dropping rocks on them . . .
Directions: Save the girl from Kong . . .

The robot sings, the games beep. There are not many human sounds. Even body language is muted. There is an adult couple at the picnic table across from me. The woman has been putting the coins into Dolly. There is a giant pepperoni and green pepper in front of them. The husband holds a roll of quarters.

"Want some pepperoni?" the woman asks. "My kids won't stop playing to eat."

I turn her down, but she takes a slice of my vegetarian special.

"It's a crazy place," she says, "but it sure beats cooking and cleaning up. Anyway, the kids love it."

"I liked it better," I tell her, "when there were place mat mazes instead of electric games."

"Me too," the husband says, "except for Asteroids. I play that to keep me sharp in business. It teaches aggressiveness. Out there, it's dog eat dog."

The dog on the wall, Jasper Jowls, growls at us.

Sam brings me sixteen tickets that he has won at Skee-ball. Each time he wins at the 25-cent game he gets two tickets worth 1 cent each when redeemed at Jasper's General Store. He gives me the booty, then he and Brad make a run for Night Driver, where they can sit together and drive 100 miles an hour through the Swiss Alps in winter.

I leave the couple and take Sam's tickets to Jasper's General Store. For the sixteen tickets I get myself a plastic back scratcher and a key chain. The girl who works behind the counter is named Laura. She advises me to become a member of the Chuck E. Cheese fan club.

"You get a ten-percent discount on everything in the store if you join, and all you have to do is give us your name and address and your birthday."

I hesitate. The children and I are already members of the birthday club at Baskin-Robbins.

A serious-looking man holding a clipboard stands against the wall. He recommends that I join. "It is a good deal," he says. "It will save you about two-forty a month."

"How do you know?"

He introduces himself as Doug Horn, a financial analyst from Merrill Lynch.

"A lot of us are keeping an eye on Pizza Time and"—he whispers it—"Show Biz. Both are publicly owned corporations that cater to the older segment of the under-ten set. You'll probably return once a month and spend twenty-four dollars each time," he says, "plus at least one of your children will have a birthday party here and maybe a preschoolers' picnic. So you see the fan club card is a good idea.

It's also handy for identification." He shows me his. I join and put the card next to my driver's license.

Doug and I go back to Dolly's piano bar for a beer. I put the quarter in this time and enjoy a little thrill knowing that her computerized heart hums for me.

Doug used to specialize in oil-field equipment, but when that market softened he was reassigned.

"I usually am a step ahead of the public. I'm a kind of futurist, but in this business the kids lead us all. They love the animals and the games. The parents will spend on anything the kids love. There hasn't been this kind of hard investment in idolatry since the days of the pharaohs."

"Is there really a Nolan Bushnell?" I ask.

"Sure. You ought to see the original store in San Jose. That's where they have Chuck E. Cheese University, mandatory for all would-be managers. It's a very effective educational device. They're thinking of franchising the trade school idea too, so there could be Chuck E. Cheese Universities everywhere, teaching you to operate all sorts of turnkey franchises. It's a great concept for Third World merchandising."

Doug is excited; for a year or two this will be good for his business. But my business, being a father, is less cyclical. I can't recoup losses and I can't be reassigned. I also don't know how to measure returns. There are a lot of intangibles, like the memory right now, brief as an electric blip, that my little girl, drawing an audience around her Pac-Man machine, not so long ago used to rub mashed bananas all over herself. I am weighed down by my inventory.

Doug is telling me that the entertainment industry is recession-proof. I am imagining that Jessica, Sam, and I are seated around an oak table at a very quiet country inn. The only animals are moose heads over the fireplace. My two, like the British children in old movies, trap the heavy napkins in their laps and ask important questions about the nature of the world as I revel in the wisdom of fatherhood.

In the midst of this post-industrial revolution I find myself wishing that Thomas Edison had lived in vain and that Nolan Bushnell had made his millions selling orthopedic shoes door to door. I want my children to eat with me, talk to me. I want them at least to explain the fascination of these flashing lights for which they desert me immediately. I want to know the opposition that is making me obsolete at 25 cents a crack.

"The idea of all the games," Doug says, "is attack or be attacked. It's the threshing floor of capitalism."

"In restaurants," I tell Doug, "I used to count on Jessica and Sam to behave very well. Even when they were three or four they could sit still for twenty minutes and play with the packets of sugar and the crackers. I used to tell them that if children didn't behave 'they' would throw us out. I needed that restaurant 'they.' I even used the example of their dining-out behavior to help me as a model at home. But at Pizza Time there is no 'they' that wants us to sit still. Here 'they' want us to run around and make noise."

"What does it profit a man if he sit still?" Doug asks.

I look at the pools of oil that have formed on top of my pizza.

Enter Melancholy.

Directions: Only one player at a time. Listen to middle age pump through your machinery. Worry, but still let your children do almost everything. Keep busy all the time. Stay up to date. Be as hip as you were in the sixties, when you thought communal life was coming for everyone along with economic justice and an end to racial strife, but earn a lot of money too so that you can experience the full scale of prerevolutionary pleasures.

Sam interrupts my reverie. "Daddy, I need you."

His friend Brad is crying at Skee-ball.

"I won," Brad says, "but the machine didn't give me any tickets."

"Show Biz is better," I say aloud.

An electrician is there in an instant with a screwdriver and a few semiconductors.

"Take it easy," he says, "nothing is perfect. Even in the Garden of Eden there was trouble until they got all the bugs out."

"I want my quarter back," Brad says.

The electrician gives him two tokens and two more for Sam.

"Keeping you people quiet eats into profits," he says. "Lucky that we budget for goodwill."

At Ms. Pac-Man, Jessica is hot. She has won five free games. Pac-Man and Ms. Pac-Man have met. They are in the chase. I am proud of my little girl's skill. After this, I think, will come rock 'n' roll, then sex and drugs, alienation, and the generation gap.

When her board changes colors, I try to stop the parental self-torture. I compromise with what awaits me. Maybe I'll buy them each a car, but not a penny for cocaine.

With all the noises of simulated intergalactic battle surrounding me, I start to imagine Jessica and Sam speeding away from me like hot particles in the infancy of the universe. I can still see them at the rim of the game room, but if I don't get out of here soon I'll need a radio telescope to hear a trace of my offspring in the empty cosmos.

My children, for your pleasure I've indulged this chaos long enough. Give me McDonald's and Kentucky Fried Chicken and the interstate highway system and all the antique Huts and Inns of my youth. I don't want to eat pizza with five hundred others amid state-of-the-art technology. I don't care if the Japanese stay a game or two ahead forever.

I roll up my LeRoy Neiman portrait of Chuck E. Cheese and call out your names through this makeshift megaphone. I'm tired and bored and have spent more than the $24 family average per visit. I want to put you to bed with a quiet bedtime story. It's enough that I've eaten dinner next to an electric hippopotamus and listened to World War III.

"Jessica, Sam, c'mon," I yell again, but nobody can hear me. Doug is watching Laura redeem the Skee-ball tickets, the TV monitors are flashing pizza numbers. Fifteen robots are singing in the Pizza Time Theatre.

I move close to try to lure them from their machines. They won't budge until I try.

"C'mon, Daddy," Jessica says, giving me her spot at Pac-Man. The crowd parts like the Red Sea to let me in. I have never tried before. The lights and directions flash. Jessica puts in the quarter. Full of wonder, I enter the maze.

Jessica and Sam become the cute little ghosts of this game, totally unpredictable, changing faster than I can imagine. Only by absolute concentration can I keep up with them for a few seconds. My coordination is slow, my peripheral vision poor. A chicken pecking at corn could play better than I do. Still, here I am in the middle of the game. The children wink and turn blue as they pass. I keep eating dots as if I have no other possible destiny.

"Wait, my little ones," I call out, "I'm getting tired of all this dot eating. I think I want a new career." The ghosts whiz by, obliterating me as they pass. Over and over I start and am wiped out.

I think of Mao Tse-tung beginning the journey of 10,000 miles with one step; I think of the human effort involved in getting us to the moon, that giant step for mankind. I think of Nolan Bushnell creating Pong and Atari and still having the stamina for more. I think of Dolly Dimples mating with the sincere ape at Show Biz to create a whole new generation of rock 'n' roll robots.

I still can't clear the board, even once. I gulp the power pill too fast, I forget about the escape tunnels. When I have to make split-second decisions I panic.

"Listen, kids, how about a little less immediacy. How about a childhood more like mine, with three-D comic books, the Korean War, and one-car families. Let's be a little less American. Don't forget, we're only a generation from the ghettos of Eastern Europe."

"Yid kidz created Robitron," the ghosts tell me. "We're too speedy for the past. Stop mooning over what used to be; this is electronics, not psychoanalysis. We're our own Morse code. Eat the dots, follow the directions. There is no message, stop looking. Move it or lose us."

I begin to understand that they really mean it. If I can't keep up, I will lose them and get only occasional postcards from other galaxies.

All right, my children, if this is it, so be it. If that cunning pattern that led us from the primeval ocean to outer space in only a few billion years has now focused on Pac-Man, then let me at this missing link in my development. Already I have fought off despair and loneliness and all the trouble of raising you two. While you became masters of the universe, I watched out for the monsters. Even here I see them, gloom in the salad line, disappointment on the scoreboards. Having come this far with you, I am not going to give up to an electronic game. Make way, my children. There is no fury like an avenging parent.

Enter the father, anew. This time throwing off his old powers and responsibilities, ready for the challenge of a two-dimensional game.

Enter Max, all mouth and teeth, throwing away memories as if they're dental floss, discarding ideas into the ether. Watch me, my former babies, as I go through six time warps and come out young and strong and forgetful of everything except the plastic knob at my right hand.

The lights flicker. Chuck E. Cheese swallows his buck teeth.

I come at Pac-Man with such ferocity that the dots turn to run from me. The power pills shrivel, I need no outside help.

"Hey," the electrician yells, "stop it, relax. Such pure will is blowing out all the circuits. Little kids can get hurt on the climbing giraffes, the pizzas will burn, and the cash registers will make the wrong change. Relax. Let the electricity move through you. You're not playing according to the rules."

Too late is the guardian of this place. I am fixed so wholly on the board that I forget my children and myself. The Pac-Man's beeps are the music of the spheres. The entire warehouse grows silent. My game flashes on all the TV monitors. Three hundred revelers watch my annihilation of Pac-Man.

The board does not give up easily. On its side are engineering and logic, but I am backed by common sense and the second law of thermodynamics. Chaos is in my right hand, and this is a one-handed game. I am destroying everything in my path and planting circuit breakers in the open spots so no other game will ever grow here.

The board pleads for mercy. Not just for Pizza Time and the $1.6 million per unit, the board pleads mercy on behalf of smart bombs and missiles, pocket calculators, and video recorders. IBM and the telephone company plead simultaneously for relief from the onslaught. They beg me to think of the future.

Too late, information revolution . . . too late, infinity ram chip . . . I have unrolled the power of the forgotten parent; not all the hope in all the singles clubs on earth can stop me now. If my past doesn't count, there can be no mercy for the technological future. Fair is fair.

"Daddy," Jessica whispers, "I'm scared."

The game can no longer keep score. The board has gone through all the primary colors and is now black. I am eating the darkness in large asymmetrical blobs. All the dots have gathered in the upper left corner to pray that I will relent.

"Let's go, Daddy, it's enough," Jessica says.

Sam touches my back pocket and tries to understand what is happening.

"They'll throw us out," he says.

"That argument won't help here," I remind him. "You didn't sit with me, you weren't quiet, you didn't behave, you didn't even eat. I'm not raising you to be space age electricians. I want some old-fashioned values or I destroy the place."

The board is all gone now. Random numbers chased by fear move helplessly across the glass. The hard plastic shell crumbles too. Pac-Man by Midway is dust and rubble at my feet.

Unrelentingly I move toward Robitron.

"I'm calling the police," the electrician says.

"All right," Jessica says, "I promise. Loud rock 'n' roll limited to my room, sex and drugs in moderation only, and a nice guest room for you in my house when the time comes. Is that enough? I'm only nine."

"Me too," Sam says. "I won't marry Chuck E. Cheese either. Maybe I'll marry Show Biz."

"Enough," the electrician says. "Out, all three of you."

My hands are already on Robitron.

Directions: You are the last human family. The robitrons conclude that human life is inefficient and therefore must be destroyed. Save Daddy, save Mommy, save Mickey . . .

We do not enter. Jessica and Sam pull me toward home. We will not be the last human family. Your turn.

Free Agents

M y heart went last. Trailing stray veins, pumping, still hot, and friendly and full of abject apologies, it joined the others.

This almost did me in.

"Fuck him," said my brain, and the battle lines formed.

"I," if you'll forgive me for the looseness of the term, was left with the brain, intact spinal column, and total skeleton minus only the riotous thumbs. Gone were the internal organs, three senses, and that whole complicated genetic code which the brain, surprisingly, could not lay claim to.

It was a classic strike, and I was stunned to the depths of my being by the issue itself and the speed with which it surfaced. Now, I am no Andrew Carnegie and my liver is no Eugene V. Debs. From each other we might have expected otherwise. Still, who knows? I can only tell you, in all honesty, that when it started I was as innocent as Florence Nightingale. The stomach grumbled, the kidneys ached a little. Yet, I thought I was "together." You know how it is. You live twenty, thirty years and in some very meaningful ways you get to feel used to yourself. For the stomach there's Di-Gel, for the kidneys Doan's pills. Most of the time you don't need anything. You can look in the mirror and think, He's not so bad. You learn to cope. Sometimes people tell you, You're cute, you're funny, you have a good personality. What happens is, you begin to take yourself for granted.

You say, "That's life." You take a drink, a wife, a job, a tranquilizer. Then suddenly, one sweet morning, you learn that behind your back your liver and kidneys have been plotting a revolution that makes Lenin seem as insignificant as the Spanish-American War. The liver and kidneys issue a proclamation endorsed within the day by all the internal organs.

"The so-called one-life one-body ruling," their press release reads, "has for an entire decade been based upon false medical, legal, and moral evidence. The star surgeons traipse through the land making big reputations by moving organs from one body to another. An average John Doe might have a new heart, a fresh kidney, pints of alien blood, even an engrafted tooth if the dentists have their way, and you know they will. Meanwhile, the organs are treated as so much meat.

"Before the age of transplants we took for granted the indignities placed upon our brothers the gallbladder, the appendix, the tonsils, and the intestine by the yard. No more.

"After the May 11 deadline which we are imposing, all organs, muscle, and tissue, whether initially within the Apple body or added subsequent to birth, become, as it were, free agents, capable of negotiating with any available bodies. We, the undersigned, hope for a just and speedy solution in the spirit of democratic fairness that has characterized the history of collective bargaining."

The liver and kidneys make this statement public on the morning of May 4. By midday all the major organs sign, and I face the distinct possibility that on May 11 the long-standing implicit contract between my parts and myself will become nonbinding.

I call my doctor. He contacts the legal division of the AMA. Their chief counsel suggests compulsory round-the-clock negotiation, with all parties continuing past the deadline without curtailment of services. The parts turn a deaf ear. The spleen, who quickly becomes their counsel and spokesman, says, "The AMA sucks. We're dealing with you, boss; it's you and us, sink or swim, no bureaucracy. Cards on the table."

Imagine how I feel. In a week I might literally go to pieces.

"Be heroic," says the brain, hanging tough. "Stand now or forever face the possibility of internal dissent."

"But I'm no hero."

"Neither was Achilles. The times make us all."

"He was nine tenths of a god."

"And you, mister frightened-of-everything, you are not made in the image of Pete Rozelle. Let them know who's boss. Do it once now or every day for the rest of your life."

"Why me?" I ask the spleen. "Why me when the world is full of strong men, examples for the young and credits to their races and nations? What's there to prove on Max Apple, who at his best barely makes it through a day? Why not Earl Campbell or Steve Carlton or Pelé, all heroes with heroic lungs and hearts and bladders? When you want new rules why not try them out on somebody who matters?"

"Ever heard of Brown versus Board of Education?" the spleen replies. "Brown was a nobody. It's the principle. Celebrity just confuses the issue. All important decisions are tested on nobodies."

"But spleen and all the rest of you," I plead, "honest to God, I thought until the minute I read your statement that we had been in a happy union since my conception. I never heard any complaints. How did it get this far without my knowledge?"

"You could have opened your eyes sooner," says the spleen, "but still none of us blames you. It's true, a week is not long. If you want long, go to art. Time flies. We have short productive seasons. If we said, Max, old buddy, sure we trust you, take a year or two, no hurry, we would become a disease, not an issue. And there's always the danger that in a moment of pique you might jet down to Houston and replace half of us with more docile members.

"Face up to it," the spleen says, "biology is destiny."

I begin to tremble.

"Get hold of yourself," he says, "this is not personal. We know that you're an easy target; so were all the generous slaveowners in the plantation days. Sure you're a decent fellow. In other times you might have anticipated a long uneventful life, a slow decay, even a pleasant enough senility. And we would have gone along as all our brethren of days past did, arm in arm with you toward the inorganic future.

"But you're no dummy, boss. Look where you're at. Where's the Family, the Church, the State? Now it's the body's turn to step into the twentieth century."

"And I am your stepping-stone?"

"Don't get sentimental," the brain says. He has heard enough. "Don't get sentimental with this crowd; it's just a waste of good feelings." He advises me to lie low, keep out of the negotiations altogether, leave everything to him. "Your weakness is your strength," he says. "Who wants your organs? These boys are not coming from Dave Winfield and Reggie Jackson. Face it, I'm the only one who might ever get another offer, and you know I'm not about to leave."

"We may be individually weak," says the spleen, "but we have numbers. And think of this while you're at it. Here you are, an obscure fellow with a chance to make major history. Deal with us, and together we'll become the Magna Carta of science."

I admit that I respond to such rhetoric with a kind of benign ecstasy. I am ready to give in, but the brain, my counsel, steps hard upon my instincts.

"In the crunch, they'll fold," he says, "they have to. Where else can they go? It's not as if there was another league. Collective bargaining itself," he says, "is a ridiculous misnomer in this circumstance," since he can discern no demarcation between labor and management.

"Then ask him," counters the spleen, "why he stays and the rest of us don't."

"Simple loyalty," says the brain, "coupled with good judgment and right reason."

They go on like this for hours. By May 9 I am a shambles. My friends, unaware of the struggle within myself, see only neurotic symptoms. Little do they know that the brain, whom they suspect, is my only mainstay. When I try to tell my boss that on May 11 I may find myself a new person, he thinks I have been doing meditation or est training. He commends me. "We all should do it," he says, "regularly. It keeps us from growing stale."

On the evening of May 10 I beg my brain, "Let them have the new ground rules. Reinstate the contract. Give them everything they want and more."

"Sorry," he says, "but the stakes are much higher than yourself. Give them you and they'll want everyone. Here we'll make our stand."

"I'm not the stuff of martyrdom."

"The readiness is all," he says, and my eyes, who stayed, though the tear ducts left, give one final gush at 9 P.M. on May 10.

At midnight when my organs leave, I become, in an instant, like Italy during a national strike. I am there but not there. The heart, as I've said, lingers, almost changes its mind, I think, at the last instant, but is driven along by the social pressure of both lungs.

I think that neither the parts nor I ever really thought it would come to this. Until the last instant we cling like lovers. Then, immediately we are divorced. And if you think that divorce between man and wife is a dismemberment, imagine my alienation.

"Marxist propaganda," says the brain. "No conditions can alienate a man from himself."

"But here I am, a hulk, an empty cavity. Prick me and I won't bleed."

"Stop being sentimental and get some rest," he says. "You'll need it. We're on the docket tomorrow at nine."

II

Without too much haggling, the brain and the members settle on the pituitary gland as judge. Although he resides in the brain's neighborhood, there clearly is no conflict of interest. During the week of turmoil—in fact, during my entire life, as far as I know—the pituitary has maintained a remarkably disinterested attitude toward all the commotions of human necessity. He also looks very judicial, small but long, gray at the sides, thoughtful, intensely calm.

The jury, though, is a horse of another color. The members insist that they be tried by peers, i.e., parts, and the judge quickly agrees over strenuous objection from the brain-prosecutor, who refuses to accept the analogy of blacks being tried by all-black juries. He attempts to call a well-known Gestalt psychologist as expert witness to protest the judge's ruling, but the bench turns a cold ear. After this ruling, jury selection proceeds quickly. Shelley's heart, Einstein's brain, and John Dillinger's penis along with nine less celebrated organs comprise the final jury. Einstein's brain, naturally, is chosen foreman.

Since the entire transcript will soon be available (Arno Press, a New York Times Company), I'll only give the highlights from my admittedly limited perspective. First, let me say absolutely that the brain as prosecutor and the spleen as chief defense attorney conducted themselves in a splendid legal manner. There were moments that might have been ugly, even grotesque, without good judgment on all sides. Yet, so orderly and decorous was the entire proceeding that in spite of the circumstances I could not help feeling proud of myself.

Among the many witnesses for the defense the spleen called:

Dr. Christiaan Barnard
Dave Winfield
Dr. Benjamin Spock
The heart of Luis Rodriguez
The right kidney of Alma Sands
Dr. Kenneth Eidel

The prosecution's list included:

William Shakespeare
Socrates
B. F. Skinner
Dr. Michael DeBakey
Jackie Robinson

Bowie Kuhn
Saint Thomas More
Masters and Johnson

When presented with the prosecution's witness list, the defense objects to the fact that fully one half of the state's witnesses are deceased. The court overrules the objection, since in all cases deceased parties are represented by adequate counsel. "In this instance," the judge blandly states, "life and death are not the important issues. Let us proceed."

To me they are, I want to yell at the top of my lungs, who ignore me from across the room. Since neither side calls upon me to testify, I am a mute witness to the playing out of my own destiny.

"You always are," says the brain. "Stop whining about it. If none of this had happened, you would be as ignorant of your internal self as you are now. Shut up and trust me."

I do so.

The central defense argument is clear enough. Organs have, at least in a legal sense, an existence of their own. They can survive individually when kept under proper circumstances and, furthermore, can and often are exchanged among various bodies without the consent of themselves. "In this day and age," states the spleen, "the body can no longer be considered as a whole." Dr. Barnard, taciturn, clearly uncomfortable, admits that though he does not like this kind of approach, it clearly seems to be scientifically accurate.

"When I began transplanting hearts," he says, almost apologetically, "I was young. There were those sufferers by the dozens turning blue daily before my eyes."

"If you had to do it all again," asks the prosecutor under cross-examination, "would you?"

Defense objects. Objection sustained, irrelevant question.

The prosecutor then asks if Dr. Barnard, in his vast surgical experience, has ever in his wildest fancy considered a heart as anything but an appendage to this or that body.

"Well, sir," says the good doctor, "yes, I have."

The brain asks no further questions, but the judge orders the jury removed and requests the doctor to continue.

"I don't like the direction in which this leads me, you know," Barnard states, "but I have indeed often wondered in the midst of many a chest if there was not something in this pulpy mass beyond my skillful fingers. I have thought of this at the moment of transplant and then sometimes weeks or even years later when the heart is rejected. Some scientists think that organ rejection can be overcome by drugs. Who knows?"

"You mean," interrupts the defense counsel, "that you believe that organs have a kind of free choice about their circumstances and are exercising it in spite of medical science."

The doctor nods a quiet yes.

The prosecutor is so angry that I am afraid all might turn to chaos now. But he quickly calms himself. "Who cares what that candy ass thinks," the brain whispers, hiding his anger as he looks over his notes on Dave Winfield.

None of the other defense witnesses seem to me very substantial. They range from Winfield's defense of capitalism (if only the case were that simple) to the straightforward but not very moving testimony of the Rodriguez heart and the Sands kidney that they were removed and relocated without their prior consent and were not especially content with their present location.

But, oh, when my large and dramatic brain begins to call the witnesses for the prosecution, then and only then does rhetoric flourish in the courtroom. Shakespeare, represented by Dillon & Reed, lays out our case in an oblique but universal fashion.

"Take but degree away and the bounded waters should lift their bosom higher than the shores, and make a sop of all this solid globe."

"Objection," says the spleen. "This language, fit perhaps for the stage, is but a subterfuge in these chambers. Cut out that honeyed tongue and let the mouth speak for itself."

"A strange metaphor for this defense," the judge observes; then he asks the Bard's counsel to be more direct.

In everyday language Shakespeare says, "Every ship must have a captain. Likewise, the vessel needs oarsmen, sails, cooks, porters, et al. If every oarsman thinks himself a captain, every cook a commander, then the ship, whether it be a body, a state, or the universe herself, flounders like a headless chicken."

In cross-examination the spleen asks very politely, "Mr. Bard, what do you mean by universe, or, more specifically, have you ever heard of the notion that there are endless suns?"

"The elephant hath joints but none for courtesy," says the Bard. "His legs are legs for necessity, not for flight."

"Do you believe," asks the impatient spleen, "that the earth is flat?"

"One touch of nature makes the whole world kin."

"Your Honor, no further questions. I think it is obvious that for all the eloquence expressed by this witness he is hardly able to make any serious judgments about twentieth-century phenomena."

The prosecutor, displeased by this subtle disparagement of a key witness, asks for a recess until tomorrow. The bench grants us only half an hour.

The brain, in a desperate resort to the living, calls B. F. Skinner. In a long and complicated testimony, Skinner asserts that wholes have little enough of what the defense calls "freedom" and that this scarce commodity dispersed among a horde of organs would lead to the end of all useful social behavior.

The sly spleen rises slowly to cross-examine. "Professor Skinner, would you please name that part of the human organism which you most admire."

"The brain."

"And if, professor, you were looking for pleasure centers, in say a lung or an intestine, how would you go about doing so?"

"I don't believe that these organs, by themselves, experience either pleasure or pain."

"You mean, sir, that they require the brain to translate sensory data and make judgments for them."

"Exactly."

"If it please the court," says the strutting spleen, "may I point out the great similarity between this world view and the pre-Lutheran

Christian view which held the Church, specifically the Pope, as the arbiter and judge of all moral phenomena. I hope the jury will see that Professor Skinner, a so-called modern scientist, makes precisely the same argument as the Elizabethan playwright. To accept such reasoning requires a return in science and theology to the Catholicism of the seventeenth century."

"Objection," from the prosecution.

"Sustained. The jury will ignore the defense attorney's statement."

The brain and I huddle. "This is getting very serious," he says. "I'm afraid it's all going against us."

"What will happen to me?" I ask.

"Ironic," he says, "that the prosecution is worried about the fate of its client. Must I remind you that you, sir, are the state. What happens when the Supreme Court rules against the government—does all legislation cease? Anyway, relax. I'm calling the big one now. Forget Masters and Johnson, they'll never make a dent on this jury."

The prosecution calls Socrates. A hush falls over the room. You can barely hear the lungs expand. After a long moment, Einstein's brain, risking its position in the jury, calls out, "Let's hear it for one who started us all on the road to wisdom." The courtroom bursts into spontaneous applause.

The bench gavels for order but himself joins in the standing ovation to the ancient Greek, represented by Baker, Sullivan & Vance.

When order is restored, the judge politely warns the entire room, especially the jury, against any further outbreaks. The spleen approaches the bench. "Your Honor, I request that the witness be removed before making any statement. Until the vogue of the modern existentialists, he has represented the greatest historical threat to my clients."

"Objection, Your Honor," from the brain. "Must we listen to such disparagement of a man whom all the world esteems?"

The court allows the spleen to continue but warns him to be specific. "All right, Your Honor, and ladies and gentlemen of the jury. Here you have Socrates, wisest of men, the prince of irony, the founder of the examined life which we are at this very moment most diligently proving." The spleen turns to face the witness. "How, Socrates, did you end your earthly stay?"

"Hemlock by the glass," says the calm philosopher.

"There you have it, Your Honor. This so-called 'wise man' destroyed his organs for the sake of an idea."

"Could you have escaped, Socrates?"

"Yes."

"Could you have bribed the jailers?"

"Yes."

"The jury?"

"Yes."

"And yet you chose to stay, to execute your own organs, and were content to leave us all with the mild witticism about going off to life and death and who knows which is better. Well, you proved your idea, sir, at the expense of innocent organs. For all you know, your heart was a sophist, your liver altogether aphilosophical. Letting this man testify, Your Honor, would be as absurd as appointing Charles Manson the guardian of Sharon Tate's offspring."

The judge is stunned. I don't blame him. The truth of the argument is altogether apparent. The court is silent. My heart beating across the room whimpers to me, a gesture of reconciliation. My pale organs wither in the fluorescent glare of this public place. My brain, that fertile, inexhaustible prosecutor, treads water in the silence.

"Your Honor," I state, hardly knowing what I do, "I wish to testify."

"Sit down, fool," whispers the brain. "If we lose, let's at least go out in style."

But finally I am able to ignore him. He seems no more persuasive at this moment than any of the other organs.

"What a piece of work a man is," Shakespeare calls out as I approach the witness stand to replace a bewildered Socrates as he steps down without having any chance to demonstrate his powers.

Neither the defense nor the prosecution rises to question me.

"Speak," says the judge.

"The Lord is my shepherd," I state, "and I shall not want."

"Objection," from both defense and prosecution.

The judge leans over and looks gravely at me. "You know the ground rules. If we wanted to do it this way, we wouldn't be in a court now, would we? The question, sir, is justice. Speak or forever lose your tongue."

"Ladies and gentlemen," I state, "those living and those represented by counsel, strangers, and my own vital parts. I admit it. The ball game is over. I am in violation of the antitrust laws, I am in restraint of trade, and I have monopolized myself. My brain has most valiantly been attempting to wrest victory or at least dignity throughout these proceedings. I thank him for his efforts, but no brain could successfully prosecute this case. I call the entire court to witness the fact that I now declare myself dispersed. Whatever previous legal rights I claimed to my parts or to any part of a part, including X-ray film and xerography, I now relinquish. Go, in good health and good fortune, to whomever you wish. And may each of you affix himself to a more solid and substantial spirit than I have proved to be."

"Your Honor," says the brain, "I ask the indulgence of the court. My client is no longer himself. Let the court spare us any further damage to what was once a model of sweet reason."

The gavel rings out. "Forgive me," I whisper to myself. The judge instructs the jury. They file out.

As we wait in silence, my brain ignores me, places an empty chair between us. I am, at this moment, beyond desolation. I am ready to throw in the towel but I don't know how. I am paralyzed, bereft of mind and body, yet in the midst of this crisis a strange indifferent calm overcomes me. It is the calm of the drowning man who gives up the struggle for one last pleasing glimpse of blue waters and teeming aquatic life.

The court fades. Left with nothing else, I am overwhelmed by memory. The memory of fleeting sensuality. The taste of vanilla ice cream. The sound of the national anthem and Rice Krispies. "I am what I am," I whisper. Then, my heart, the one who I know has been sympathetic throughout, steps across the bar that separates us and begins to beat within me not a millimeter from his accustomed spot.

His movement of return is stately, dignified, self-conscious, not like the hasty retreat of yesterday. He is telling me something, this heart of mine. Barely has he settled into the cavity of my chest when the others, equally austere and serene, join en masse. Kidneys, liver, thumbs, nerve endings, tear ducts, and finally the spleen himself. All these come to me as if I am gravity. The brain maintains a puzzled silence. The judge too has resumed his previous anonymity.

"I am what I am," I state again, this time more confidently, and the organs hum like an Indianapolis 500 engine. I can sense that each one of them is as happy to be back in his smooth soft spot as I am to have him there. I shift gears. I rise. I walk. I spit. I think.

"Nothing is settled," the brain reminds me. "The jury is still out."

"But," I say, "I am together again." I roar, I bellow, I beat my chest. When the jury returns glum and single file, I take a deep breath and blow them out of the box.

They scatter in my wind. "We were hung," Einstein's brain calls out from the blue sky. "And you, so recently yourself again, don't be so violent. We're all up in the air anyway."

"To tell me this," I yell to the heavens, "I don't need Einstein's brain." Clouds suck up the jury. Full of myself, on tiptoes I bounce on the grass, ready for everything.

Momma's Boy

On Saturdays Gil Stein went to three movies. It was convenient; he just picked a Cinema III, so there wasn't any driving around town. He ate popcorn and beef jerky which he carried in his pocket and sometimes ate for lunch during the week too.

His wife, Cheryl, sometimes went to the Saturday movies, but usually she stayed home or went shopping with two women friends from the Brompton Arms apartments.

In the dark at a Cinema I, II, or III, Stein felt like a soldier on limited rations. He ate the dried beef and popcorn slowly so that they would last a long time as he pretended he was trapped, surrounded on all sides with only a one-week supply of food. It would be two months before help arrived, and then only if there were no monsoons or droughts or enemies along the way or political opposition at home.

Heroically, Stein nibbled at beef and single kernels of corn while he stayed alert and never missed a beat in the plot of the movie he was watching. He liked desert movies with scenes of heat and thirst and impossible endurance. *Lawrence of Arabia* was his favorite.

Cheryl preferred musicals. Mostly there wasn't a movie showing that either of them liked, so they just went to whatever was on. Cheryl hummed the music to herself when she wanted a musical, and when he wanted a desert feeling, Stein kept himself from the water fountain after his popcorn and salted beef.

Most of his work now was connected to the Middle East. There was even a chance he might have to go there for a while. He was a specifications and drafting specialist for the Fluor Corporation. The company had over $2 billion worth of contracts in Saudi Arabia, Yemen, and the Sudan. In his office the walls were filled with pictures of the desert blooming, the desert with flowers at the tops of cacti and oases as ordinary as backyard swimming pools.

"With one word," Cheryl said, "with a single memo, you could change some things, you could make them better."

"It's not my job to change things," Stein said.

The project engineers brought him specifications for a columnar airport terminal that was supposed to look as if it floated atop the sand. They brought him hospital rooms with doors too narrow for stretchers to pass through, understressed concrete foundations, and smoky glass windows facing away from the sun. He never corrected the plans. They went through many hands. It was not up to him to save the structural integrity of the Persian Gulf.

"I'm paid to be a draftsman," he told Cheryl. "That's all I'm going to be."

"But if you corrected some of those things, wouldn't they give you a promotion?"

"No," Stein said. "You get promoted for doing your work and letting someone else do theirs. Live and let live is my philosophy."

When a walkway collapsed in a hotel in Kansas City killing more than a hundred people, Cheryl accused him.

"That wasn't our project."

"You know what I mean. A lot of somebodies let that one get by too."

She went to her room to cry. She cried for the victims in Kansas City, but it took no tragedy to bring Cheryl Stein to tears. She cried on cloudy days and on bright days for good reason or for no reason.

She cried, Stein finally realized, because it was as natural for her as eating or talking. It bothered him, but he stopped paying attention. She tried her best to stop. She went to behavior modification class. Once she even bought a battery-operated unit designed to give her an electric shock every time moisture reached her cheeks. She walked around the house with electrodes glued on either side of her nose. She gave up because it went off accidentally too many times.

"I learned," she told Stein, "that wet cheeks happen a lot in a kitchen. Anyway, the electrode jelly was giving me pimples."

At work, Stein's friends, one by one, were being sent to the desert. Nobody joked about it. People chipped in for expensive but necessary gifts like video recorders and a great many books. The salary was high and included a four-week paid vacation in the United States at the end of eighteen months. Solemn engineers went off like teenage draftees.

"I don't think they'll send me," Stein told Cheryl. "I'm not important enough." Sometimes watching her cry he thought he wouldn't mind being in the desert.

Sadness was written all over Cheryl's life. Her childhood photographs were framed by tears. Cheryl in the tree house crying, Cheryl hugging a Barbie with a wet bodice, Cheryl at camp with tears dripping from her even while she smiled for the group picture.

On their wedding night she sobbed.

"You're not a virgin," Stein said playfully. "What's there to cry about?"

"You fool," Cheryl said, "that's why I'm crying." Stein's wavy hair fell into deep curls from her tears during lovemaking. In Saudi Arabia, he thought, she'd be a natural resource.

During *Hair,* Stein walked out on his wife. A month or so before, they had seen *Grease* and liked it but he couldn't stand *Hair* and Cheryl refused to leave. He felt a little strange that night, as if he was extra aware of things. The music was too loud, the movements on the screen too jerky. In the men's room at the Majestic Theatre he had a revelation. It was a very old bathroom with head-high urinals that enclosed the user. There were tiny cracks of age all through the porcelain but it was so bright at the top, so well polished and clean, that looking straight ahead Stein saw himself instead of graffiti. Looking at his vague reflection in that immense urinal, Stein felt overwhelmed by the urge to escape. He did not ever want to see the rest of *Hair,* he did not ever want to see Cheryl. He could just walk away. The idea exhilarated him. He pissed on his shoe.

Later that evening Stein returned to their apartment but the battle lines were drawn. Cheryl was awake in bed looking at the *National Geographic.*

"I think we should get divorced," she said.

"All I did was walk out of a movie."

"But it's the way we are about everything," Cheryl said. "We've been married for four years and I don't know what you're like. I would look foolish on one of those couples quiz shows. We eat together and we sleep together and we have a joint checking account, but is this living together?"

Her eyes were dry.

II

The parting was easy. They used a lawyer who advertised in the TV booklet of the Sunday paper, $149 uncontested. Cheryl worked for three lawyers but she didn't want them to know her personal business. Only a few weeks before *Hair,* Cheryl and Stein had gone out to dinner with the three lawyers and their wives and the other two legal secretaries and their husbands. At dinner one of the lawyers made a toast, "to the three best secretaries and their new Apples." All they talked about was computers. Stein thought they should have had the machines at the table too.

They all ate steak and lobster. It was a steak and lobster restaurant. Stein watched everyone eat.

"You're embarrassing me," Cheryl whispered. "Stop staring."

The lawyers, he noticed, chewed on the right sides of their mouths, the secretaries on their left. Stein thought that he varied from side to side. He wondered aloud if people tended to favor one side for chewing, but nobody took up the question.

"What do you think of the word processor?" Cheryl's boss asked him.

"I think it will chew up the work," Stein said.

On Monday Cheryl's boss told her, subtly, she said, that he felt sorry for her being married to a creep who stared at people while they ate.

"I defended you," Cheryl said. She cried for ten minutes while she cooked instant mashed potatoes and made a salad. Stein barbecued their hamburgers on a hibachi no bigger than his shoe. He promised never to embarrass her like that again. He did not watch Cheryl chew. He looked instead at her small white throat, at her Adam's apple hidden beneath the soft flesh but spurting away now and then like a secret heart.

Stein took the Camaro, Cheryl got everything else. It was a fair split. He thought he might not be able to sit through movies anymore after walking out of *Hair* and all that it led to. He thought he would feel guilty.

But Stein felt no guilt. He didn't think of Cheryl that much. He subleased a one-bedroom condominium from one of the people transferred to the Middle East. He went out now and then with one of the girls from the office. She gave him an orange tabby cat. Stein thought he was getting along very well. Thus he was totally surprised when he started beating his mother.

Mrs. Stein was a small woman who took a punch well. She had a square, determined jaw, but her son rarely hit her in the face.

"I never beat Cheryl," he wondered aloud, "I don't kick the cat. I don't hit anybody else."

Though the blows hurt her, Mrs. Stein was grateful for the attention. A widow alone in the world aside from her only child, she lived on a quiet street. A single scream would have brought many neighbors. Police, judges, social workers, the whole system would have been at her side if only her throat would open for one desperate second.

She had a clear and loud voice, too, and had performed as a soloist in her high school glee club. She was not shy nor was she afraid of the embarrassment. Marilyn Stein's picture was in the paper once for chasing and catching the teenager who had snatched her purse. She caught him at a red light. The young thief was afraid of crossing against heavy traffic. She slapped his face and pulled her purse back. The young man apologized. His picture was in the paper too. No charges were filed.

After he hit her the first time, Stein cried. "Forgive me, Mom," he wailed. He had hit her a left jab to the shoulder. She fell to the couch. Her right shoe knocked down one of the bentwood side chairs.

"It's all right," she said. She cradled his head in her arms as she had when he was a child. He wondered suddenly why he had never held Cheryl this way during her sojourn in the vale of tears.

When Cheryl cried he touched her hair, he brought her Kleenex, a glass of water, he tried to wait it out. Finally he would just go into the other room to watch TV, or if she was crying in front of the TV he would go into the bedroom to read his sports magazines.

Cheryl did not have to be unhappy to cry, and Stein did not have to be angry to hit his mother.

Cheryl always stopped within half an hour. "Forgive me," she said, "I don't know what came over me."

That was exactly what he told his mother.

"It's OK," Mrs. Stein said. "Boys have a feisty spirit."

Stein was thirty-two years old and had never had a feisty spirit. It would have interfered very much with his work if he had such a spirit. He was good because he was not feisty.

"I think I wanted to hit Cheryl lots of times but I never did." He told this to his mother by way of apology.

"It's all right," she said again. "It's better to hit a mother than a wife. Maybe your next wife will be someone you can hit, or even explain your feelings to so you won't have to hit."

"Mom, I don't want to be a wife beater. Don't you understand how bad I feel?"

"You're not a wife beater. This is different. You're alone and frustrated. You have to be angry at someone. If you hadn't hit me maybe you would have attacked a woman on the street or molested a child. Maybe you would be suicidal.

"There are worse things than hitting your mother." She stretched and reached over to pat his head. Stein hit her a left to the midsection, a right to the ribs, and then an openhanded combination to the right cheek. The old lady crumpled at his feet. She whimpered silently. Stein lifted her to her feet, apologized, then went to see *Gone With the Wind* in 70 millimeter.

He started to wonder if she was right. Maybe he could attack women on the street or molest children. Maybe the decent draftsman moviegoer had a pervert's soul. Maybe Stein in line for refreshments would explode like popcorn into seventeen personalities, maybe the quiet of his daily life was only an illusion. Cheryl used to accuse him of lack of feeling. "I cry," she would say. "What do you do?"

Sometimes Stein had answered her accusations. "I ache too," he said. "I want a child and a wife who'll talk to me and go to ball games with me and I want a better job. . . . I want the Dodgers to win the pennant and I want you to stop the goddamn tears all the time. I feel like I'm living in a swamp."

Whenever he had answered her she cried. He learned to listen silently. Still, most of the time even when he was silent she had sobbed into a lace handkerchief.

He wondered if it was his very presence that made her cry so much. He called Cheryl from the phone booth outside the Majestic after *Gone With the Wind*.

"Cheryl, do you cry without me? Was living with me what made you cry so?"

She hesitated. "I don't think so," she said. "I've got to go now." As she hung up, Stein thought he heard a wail go through the telephone.

He stood outside the empty theater watching himself to see if he would molest anyone. He checked to see if there was blood under his fingernails or signs of a struggle in his apartment.

"I'm not a violent man," he said aloud to himself. "Why did I hit my mother?"

For two months he hung up whenever his mother called. He did not respond when she started to write letters. He returned unopened the robe she sent for his thirty-third birthday.

One day Cheryl was at his door. Outside it was raining heavily. The streets were so dark and deserted it reminded him of the newsreels of London during the Blitz.

Stein invited her in. They had not seen each other since the divorce hearing.

"How are you, Cheryl?"

"I'm getting along." In one swift glance she noticed his cat, his drapes, the new couch and chair.

"Your mother asked me to come," Cheryl said. "She is worried because you are out of touch."

"What else?"

Cheryl looked puzzled. "Nothing else. She wants to see you, she wants to know that you're alive and well, that's all. Is that asking so much?"

"Since when are you a defender of my mother?"

"Look," Cheryl said, "I did not come here to fight."

She spoke slowly, pronouncing each syllable.

"I'm trying to keep my emotions under control. It's not easy to visit you. I'm doing so as a humanitarian deed."

Stein remembered Cheryl marching through the apartment complex to collect for the Leukemia Society. She put in many hours but never gave a nickel herself.

Stein noticed that Cheryl took deep yoga breaths. She sat very straight in the chair too. Stein asked about the breathing.

"It's a method of control. I go to classes and listen to tapes at home. I'm trying to stop the tears."

She almost faltered on the word. Stein was proud of the way she caught herself, paused for a deep one, and went on.

"You were not responsible for my tears, you must know that, but you were often very cruel. I'm sorry I didn't tell you that when you called. You were cruel in ways you probably never realized."

"But I never hit you," Stein said.

"Do you wish now that you had?"

"I don't know," Stein said. "I wanted to hit you lots of times when you were in the bedroom crying. I wanted to hit you or shake you or do something to get you to stop."

"But you never did."

"How do you hit someone who's already crying?"

"It might have shown that you cared."

"I cared. Now I'm hitting my mother."

"Oh, God," Cheryl said. "Hard?"

"Not hard. Openhanded. I've only done it twice but it scares me."

"Oh, God," she said again, "you poor tortured man. Maybe you hate women."

"I like women," Stein said. "I don't even hate my mother."

"Did she overprotect you when you were young?"

"Of course," Stein said. "You know I'm an only child. You know my father died when I was eleven. Protecting me was her main occupation. But she was a good mother. She worried that I would get diabetes or stroke or cancer of the colon. When I was a teenager she treated me as if I was an old man."

"You seemed old to me too while we were married. You were always kind of thoughtful and withdrawn. I don't think I ever saw you excited."

"It was hard to be excited while you were crying."

"I deserve that," she said. "I know I was a mess. My parents never gave me any confidence. I was not ready for marriage. I should have worked, taken care of myself, lived alone for a while."

Stein noticed that his wife, now no longer his wife, was a plain-looking woman in a gray wool coat. The rain had plastered her hair on her forehead. A puddle formed beneath her. He did not remember ever having loved her, and the years of their married life were less vivid to him than the high school prom in *Grease.* He knew that they met and went to the movies a few times and made love and pretty soon she was ordering a dress with a hoop skirt and he rented a tuxedo and they got blood tests and he thought somehow that life was really about to get started.

Cheryl's eyes looked nice now that they were dry. He wanted to ask her if she had ever had her wisdom teeth removed and if her periods were more regular now and if she still watched Miss America with a scorepad beside her. Though he did not remember love, he recalled these things and the way she clenched a barrette between her teeth while she brushed her thick hair from the bottom.

"I don't know why I hit my mother," he said. "It's odd."

When the rain stopped Cheryl left, unharmed by her former husband.

Stein's transfer to Riyadh surprised him even though for months people in his department had been cleaning their desks and packing up. Some refused and looked for new jobs, but jobs were scarce and the money was very good. If he stayed three years, Stein knew he could come back with enough cash to buy a house or maybe even start his own small drafting business. But it would seem like three years in Siberia.

He phoned his mother to tell her. He didn't particularly want to talk to her, but there was nobody else. She insisted that he come over. Stein went, promising himself that he would go to a psychiatrist if he hit her again.

Mrs. Stein served her son a dinner of London broil and asparagus tips. She had tears in her eyes.

"If you go to Arabia I'll be all alone."

"Mom," he said, "you should be glad to get rid of me. Look what I'm doing, I'm hitting you. I'm not a good son, you should be glad to get rid of me."

"Don't say such a thing," she said. "No mother wants her child to leave. Three years is a long time. I'm already sixty-seven."

"Mom," he said, "it's my work, my career, my life. I don't have anything else." He realized as he said it that it was true, he didn't have anything else. All those flimsy plans in the desert, they were the structures of his life. He started to think of the silent veiled ladies of Arabia and the desert wind. He steeled himself for the coming ordeal the way movie characters lost in the desert always did. Someday he would find distant hills, civilization, water. Someday, he hoped, there would be more than this.

"First you walk out on your wife," his mother said, "and then you beat me and leave me to die alone while you go to build schools for Arab shepherds."

"I have to, Mom." Stein was ready to explain again the dreary scope of his life.

His mother's left hook caught him beneath the eye. Her engagement ring made a deep gash, and he felt his eye begin to swell at once. He had no desire to return the punch.

Even though his pain was severe and blood rolled into his mouth, Stein laughed.

"All right, Mom, we're even."

"Not even," she said. "Watch out wherever you'll be, watch out. I still owe you a few."

Business Talk

James and I have been worrying about things. I'm
bored, restless, and in late afternoon always depressed. He tries to be helpful. The children are not too bad. My
education is more than adequate. I understand what's happening as
it happens. Still, I'm powerless. At four I get morose, by five I am
tearful. When James comes home I look as if I've been pinched by
devils all day long.

"Every day is driving me crazy," I say. "I don't want to fall victim
to the malaise of the times."

"You need to get out. You need to do something. A job," he says.

"What about a business?" I say. "Something small enough to
afford, big enough to make me proud of my achievement and aware
of my responsibility."

James is a solid man. Around him I shouldn't be so sad. "I'm open
for anything," he says. "Give it a try. But first let's get down to brass
tacks." We discuss insecurity, the care of the children, guilt, the
dinner hour, vacations, the minimum wage, tax brackets, the effects
of the climate on perishables, growing old, profits, and free time.

"What the hell," James says, "small business made this country. I'm with you one hundred percent."

I call my friend Jeannie, who wants to be my partner. She has no children but is going crazy anyway. In Peru, where she grew up, there was always a clutch of servants to iron her pure cotton clothes. Here, she has no help and can't get used to permanent press. Everything she wears is heavily starched. You can hear her fabrics moving down the hall.

"I'll be a partner to anything," she says. "My father grew up on the pampas of Argentina. He skinned cattle and walked among bulls. I can't go two blocks from my apartment without worrying about some black man cutting my throat. Also, being out in the world will improve my English. We have two thousand dollars saved for a Christmas trip to Peru. I'll risk it."

"What about Bill?" I ask.

"He doesn't want to go anyway. He is just going along to please me. He would rather go to a convention in Las Vegas. I'll save him two hundred dollars."

I talk about renting a space in the Gypsy Market, and then just before the health inspector comes I dream that I find the rotting carcass of a dog underneath the sink. I know even in the dream that it is the same dog I have been seeing for weeks at the corner of University and Greenbriar when I jog past every morning right after carpool. I've called the city four times but nobody picks up the body. So now that dog enters my dreams and makes me apprehensive about going into business.

James laughs it off. I remind him about Caesar's wife. "Literary references," he says, "belong in the classroom, not the real world. Anyway, Caesar's dream was life and death. Yours is just about a health certificate. If necessary you can bribe the inspector."

"I'd never do that," I say.

"In business sometimes you have to resort to the underhanded. Wait. You'll see."

Jeannie calls and is nervous. I will go it alone if necessary. She is strengthened by my resolve. We decide to gather as much information as possible and talk to a lawyer before we sign a lease. Jeannie wants us to be a corporation with stationery and a logo. I spend the early morning calling long distance until I find out that there is a distributor right here in Houston. I leave my name.

At ten, Norman the food distributor answers my message. "You can still jump in early," he says. "Frozen yogurt is going to vanquish ice cream. It's got the texture of Dairy Queen, the taste of Baskin-Robbins, and is loaded with vitamins and beneficent bacteria. There's also low start-up costs and a product that has a fifteen-day fresh life. That's a hell of an advantage in the food business. Ice cream loses flavor after a week no matter what the temperature. And Dairy Queen never has any taste to begin with. You ought to be able to clear a hundred a day just about anywhere."

He makes an appointment to come over in an hour.

Jeannie is too nervous to meet him. "Take notes," she tells me. She has always done badly at job interviews and doesn't want to jinx our business. She thinks it's because her English turned bad in Peru. "You be the public relations person," she says. "I'll do a traffic survey of the location."

Norman brings me a sample, strawberry, in a little carton. It has melted. I put it in my freezer. We await its return to form.

"I didn't know you were this young and attractive," Norman says. "Most of the housewives who want to go into the restaurant business are old ladies hoarding some secret recipes that they think will make them rich. It's nice to see young mothers getting into the business world. Who will take care of your kids?"

"You too?" I say.

"Wait a minute, don't get me wrong." He runs to his station wagon, returns with a paperback copy of *Playing Around: Women and Extramarital Sex*. He touches my breasts and tries to move me to-ward the couch. "It gives people confidence to know they are desired," he says. "It's good business psychology."

I go to the freezer for my product. It's not bad. "A little too sugary," I tell him.

"We've got to sugar it. Bacteria is bitter. The health nuts and anti-sugar people are only a tiny fraction of the market. Believe me, we've got the data. Only fifteen percent of the population has tasted yogurt. But in this new shape it will hit everyone. This will do to ice cream what television did to radio."

Norman is about forty. He talks quickly. I know that he would scare Jeannie.

James calls to tell me that he is deeply involved with the Saudi Arabians and may have to go to Antarctica. "It sounds crazy but they want to move an iceberg to the Middle East. They can't drink oil, and they think this may be cheaper than desalinization. Who knows? Anyway, they want us to do a feasibility study. I'll be in charge. It's a twelve-million-dollar contract but I'll have to spend two months in Antarctica.

"Don't change your plans," he says, "everything will work out." He has to take the Saudi Arabians to lunch. "They love the topless places but in the long run it saves money. A few years ago you would have had to take them to whorehouses in bad neighborhoods."

"I'm going to the Statue of Liberty Bank at one thirty," I tell him, "to inquire about a loan. I hear that they're receptive to female entrepreneurs."

"I'll be at the Boobie Rock just across the street," he says. "Peek your head in if you have a chance."

Norman offers to accompany me to the bank. "I'll help you sell them on the idea of frozen yogurt as the backbone of a little natural-food dessert shop. You've got everything going for you. They'd be nuts to turn you down for a small loan." While I drive, Norman tries to rub my leg. "I have to spend most of my days with men," he says. "Getting women into the business world is the best thing that could happen. After all day in the office I'm too tired for my wife. If she could just be there at noon dressed as a waitress, our marriage would be much better." He wants me to tell him everything about James. He is even envious of Antarctica. "Food is OK," Norman says, "but the real money is in heavy things. If you need cranes and a lot of equipment, then it's easy to hide costs. I'm hoping for a job as a steel salesman; that's where the money is. When you sell tons rather than cases, you're in the big time. Jesus, you've got wonderful legs. I love to watch your muscle when you hit the brake."

At the Statue of Liberty Bank, Mrs. Fern Crawford, V.P., talks turkey to the ladies.

"Face it, sister," she says, "you're talking about a one- or two-woman operation. A three-thousand-dollar machine and a kinky product. On the next block are thirty-one flavors, the Colonel, and Roy Rogers, with Jack-in-the-Box and Burger King within walking distance. Who's going to blow a buck twenty-nine on frozen yogurt with wheat germ and sesame toppings, followed by herbal tea and a fortune cookie?"

"Everybody," Norman answers. "We're already in malls and supermarkets from coast to coast. We're moving in institutions and package sales as well."

Fern Crawford taps her heel with her pen. "Still, it's a fad."

"So was lipstick," Norman reminds her, "and the Frisbee."

"Frankly, we're looking for women who want to go into previously all-male areas like auto parts. Just this morning I approved a woman for tool rental, and a former elementary school music teacher for an electroplating shop. Fast food has had its day." Still, she says that tomorrow they'll loan me $3,000 using my IBM stock as collateral.

When we leave I walk across the street to see if James is in the Boobie Rock. I see absolutely naked girls carrying trays. The three Arabs are in traditional dress. James isn't there.

"These expense account guys have it made," Norman says. "When I take someone to lunch it's at Taco King, and that bitch tells you fast food is dead. God, how'd you like to eat here every day, with all that stuff watching you? Still, I like you lots better. I prefer serious people."

Jeannie has been talking to David Simmons, our prospective landlord. He remodeled an old house in barn wood and has turned it into a tiny mall and restaurant. His wife left him last month. He lives in the attic and eats his meals in the restaurant. We think we could get his restaurant customers to buy our frozen yogurt for dessert.

David wrings his hands. He is always worried. Two gay cooks and a waiter run his restaurant. They are constantly arguing. They buy their ingredients fresh every day. David drives across town to the

Farmers' Market for the vegetables. He has already had three minor accidents on the freeway. When he returns they stop arguing and cook whatever he buys. The staff all hate David for his inefficiency. His wife hates him because he is not successful. In the attic he caught gonorrhea from a waitress who was converting to Judaism.

"You can have a room for a hundred and twenty-five dollars a month, one-year lease, first and last month in advance, and you're responsible for all improvements." Jeannie writes down the terms. She thinks her ties to the Spanish community will also bring in a little business. David Simmons thinks we would be smarter to open a gem and mineral business. "I know an absolute dummy who made fifty thousand his first year in a store as big as a shoebox. But he didn't pay any taxes and they took it all away." David's wife is suing him for everything. "She'll probably evict me from the attic," he says.

There are already two potters named Bob, a leather worker, and a Scandinavian importer in the Gypsy Market. David himself sweeps the floors and does the general maintenance. He wants to put an art gallery in the dark hallway. People complain that there is only one restroom and everyone has to stand in line during the noon rush.

"I don't like it," Jeannie says. She thinks we would do better to pay more rent for a better spot. Bill thinks so too.

James comes home with the three Arabs. For the children they bring a two-foot wooden figure of King Faisal. For me a digital watch with an Islamic face. The children run wild, break the figurine, eat, take a bath, and are in bed by seven thirty. Alma goes home at seven twenty. She waits for her bus in the rain. The Arabs want James to leave for Antarctica next week. They have plane tickets hidden in their loose robes. James tells them about my plans for a small tea-room featuring frozen yogurt. The idea of freezing anything makes them talk more about Antarctica.

When they leave in a yellow cab I tell James all about Norman and the business possibilities.

"Men are like that," he says. "They aren't prepared to treat you as an equal in business. It will take another generation. You are in the forefront."

I tell him that Norman has been fondling me.

"Typical salesman," he says. The Arabs have been driving him crazy buying souvenirs of Texas. He will have to buy a winter wardrobe tomorrow. He doesn't even know where in Houston to look for arctic gear. He will call Neiman-Marcus in the morning.

I shower, shave my legs, and begin to read the book Norman gave me. Jeannie calls to say that maybe we should take the Gypsy Market location after all. Not doing anything for all these months has probably warped her judgment, she thinks. Bill suggests that we both take a course in real estate.

In the morning after Jessica goes to school and Alma takes the baby for a walk, I sit down to think things over. I think about how I sat through all those awful hours of school and college, how I fell in love with James and several others, and how quickly the children are growing. I wonder if a business will make me a more responsible person. I check my navel to see if that dark line down my middle that appeared after Sam was born has become any fainter. James calls it the equator. Dr. Thompson says it is perfectly normal but I don't think I'll ever wear a bikini again.

Jeannie has a friend who is a lawyer. He specializes in charity work and will check our lease for $125. She and Bill now think that even if the business doesn't earn any profit, it will be a good experience for both of them. I wear my new Italian T-shirt and soft flannel slacks. When I get to the Gypsy Market the cooks are already unpacking the vegetables from David's car. Jeannie and David are talking about the lease. At ten thirty Norman arrives looking for me. "I can't stand it," he says. "All I did last night was think of you. My wife thinks I'm coming down with a cold. I had to take a sleeping pill." He and David talk about the restaurant business and retailing in general. Jeannie's friend, the lawyer, meets us for lunch and looks over the standard contract. "Are you making any money here, Simmons?" he asks David.

"I'm making money, but what good is it?" David says. He wrings his hands. "I haven't seen my kids in three weeks."

"I'm going before the parole board this afternoon on behalf of a man who hasn't seen his kids in eleven years," the lawyer says. We all have spinach salad and eggplant Parmesan. David doesn't offer

to treat as a gesture of goodwill. Norman suggests it. Jeannie and
I sign the lease, then David tells the waitress to give him the check.
Jeannie gives the lawyer a $125 personal check. Norman orders a
bottle of champagne. We go into the room that will be ours. As a
surprise Norman has already put the frozen yogurt machine on the
counter. It is about twice the size of a microwave oven and is shiny
as a mirror. Jeannie is so excited that she kisses the bright surface and
says "I love you" in Spanish to the machine. We all drink a toast.

"To a new life and a new business," Norman says.

"Actually," the lawyer says, "a corporation is a legal individual.
You really should be a corporation."

I call James at the office. He is already wearing a sealskin coat over
a down jacket just to see how it feels. He congratulates me and
sounds excited for us.

Norman wants to come home with me. For the time being I put
him off. Jeannie is already planning the decoration of the room.

At night when the children are asleep and James has put away his
atlas, when I've washed my face with Clinique and he has clipped
his fingernails and we estimate if we have any energy for each other
after all the activity of the day, I ask him if he ever thought that I
had any talent for business and whether he considered me a frivolous
person who is just going from one thing to the next in constant
search of release from the boredom of daily life, which shouldn't be
so boring, should it?

He is thumbing through my book, reading courtesy of Norman
about the extramarital adventures of twenty-six New York women
over a fifteen-year period.

He looks up from extramarital adventure. The frozen tundra is on
his mind. He scratches his chin. I wrap my arms around my knees.
Next month he'll be at the bottom of the earth and I will be an
entrepreneur, making change.

"You want a business," he says. "I want a yacht and sunshiny
carefree days. Jeannie wants good diction. The Arabs want topless
girls and an iceberg. Everyone wants somebody else's husband and
wife and all their possessions. And the kids are the worst cannibals
of all."

"It's true," I say, thinking already of gingham tablecloths and big stacks of dollar bills stuffed into the blue sacks that the bank gives to business people. "I'm excited," I say, "but apprehensive about everything. I could lose the money or run off with Norman, or begin to bicker with Jeannie, or neglect the children. And you might get the comforts you want in Teheran or Riyadh and send me a meager alimony. Lots might happen when I leave the house."

"Business is business," he says. We sigh like cats.

I get the lubricant, he the prophylactics. Sometimes we're old-fashioned people doing the best we can.

Post-Modernism

I t's always safe to mention Aristotle in literate company. I have known this since my freshman year in college. Furthermore, that esteemed philosopher by praising Homer for showing rather than telling gave all storytellers forever after the right to stop being philosophers whenever it suits us, which is most of the time.

So, invoking sacred Aristotle and having no theory to tell, I will show you a little post-modernism. Alas, I have to do this with words, a medium so slow that it took two hundred years to clean up Chaucer enough to make Shakespeare, and has taken three hundred years since then to produce the clarity of Gertrude Stein. Anyway, I confess that we writers are as bored as any other artists. We get sick of imitating the old masters, the recent masters, and the best sellers. We are openly jealous of composers who can use atonal sounds, painters who experiment with xerography and sculptors with Silly Putty and polyester. Other makers of artistic objects have all this new technology, not to speak of color, and here we are stuck with the rules of grammar, bogged down with beginnings, middles, and ends, and constantly praying that the muse will send us a well-rounded lifelike character.

As an exercise, let's imagine a character who is a contemporary writer. He has read Eliot and Proust and Yeats and even had a stab at *Finnegans Wake.* He is well acquainted with the Oxford English Dictionary and Roget's Thesaurus. There he is sitting before his word processor thinking, What will it be today, some of the same old modernist stuff, a little stream-of-consciousness perhaps with a smattering of French and German? Or maybe he looks out the window, notices the menacing weather, and thinks, This will be a day of stark realism. Lots of he saids and she saids punctuated by brutal silences.

As he considers epiphanies, those commonplace events that Joyce put at the heart of his aesthetic, our writer scans the morning paper. This is a research activity. In the trivial he will find the significant, isn't that what art is all about?

So the writer looks, and it is astonishingly easy. There it is, the first gift of the muse. One column quotes Colonel Muammar Qaddafi of Libya stating that his nation is ready to go to war against the United States. Directly across the page an ad for Target Stores pictures a Texas Instruments pocket calculator, regularly $9.97: "today only" $6.97, battery *included.*

The writer is stunned. He has followed this particular calculator since its days as a $49.95 luxury. He has seen it bandied about by Woolco and K-Mart and, under various aliases, by Sears, Penney's, and Ward's. Never has it been offered with the battery included. This is something altogether new. He remembers Ezra Pound's dictum, "Make it new." Still there is the possibility of an error, a misprint, a lazy proofreader, a goof by the advertising agency— plenty of room for paranoia and ambiguity, always among the top ten in literary circles. And the sad thing is, this particular ad will never appear again. Qaddafi will be quoted endlessly, but the sale was "today only." This is one of the ambiguities the writer has to live with.

Of course our writer doesn't equate Target and the battery to war and peace, not even to the United States and Libya. He hardly considers the nuance of the language that uses the same terms for commerce and war: "Target," "battery," "calculate"—he can't help it if the language is a kind of garbage collector of meanings. All he wants to do is know for sure if that nine-volt battery is really included. He can, if he has to, imagine a host of happy Libyans clutching their $6.97 calculators and engaged in a gigantic calculating bee against the U.S., a contest that we might consider the moral equivalent of war and save everyone a lot of trouble.

His imagination roams the Mediterranean, but the writer will suppress all his political and moral feelings. He will focus absolutely on that calculator and its quizzical battery. He will scarcely notice the webbed beach chair peeking out of the next box or the sheer pantyhose or any of the other targeted bargains.

Let's leave our writer for a moment with apologies to Aristotle and begin to do a bit of analysis. Of course you have known all along that I have been trying to demonstrate a "post-modern" attitude. Maybe you would characterize this attitude as a mixture of world weariness and cleverness, an attempt to make you think that I'm half kidding, though you're not quite sure about what.

But even in this insignificant example nothing quite fits. It should be easy. We have only one character, the writer. He was sitting before his word processor and reading the paper. He was not described, so you assumed, no doubt, that it was me.

You were wrong. I don't even know how to type and am allergic to word processors. Furthermore, I have never read a thesaurus and I do my work standing at a Formica-topped counter.

The writer I was talking about was Joyce Carol, a young widow supporting quintuplets by reviewing books for regional little magazines. Her husband died in a weight-lifting accident. Her quints were, you have already guessed, the chemical outcome of what for years had seemed a God-given infertility. Joyce Carol struggles to understand all the books she reviews though she could earn a better wage as a receptionist for Exxon or even selling industrial cleaners and have a company car to boot; but then who would stay home with the quints?

Poor Joyce Carol is stuck with being a book reviewer as women have been stuck at home with books and children for at least two hundred years.

She is also about to begin composing her thirty-ninth gothic romance. Ladies in fifteenth-century costume will waste away for love while men in iron garments carry fragrant mementoes of their ladies and worry about the blade of their enemy penetrating the few uncovered spots of flesh.

Joyce Carol's quints lie in a huge brass carriage. They are attended by five Vietnamese wet nurses and a group therapist.

There is a photographer from the *National Enquirer* doing an in-depth story on the drug that gave Joyce Carol her quints. He is blacking out fingers and toes on the babes and asking the wet nurses to look forlorn.

Joyce Carol used to write exquisite stories of girls who couldn't decide whether they truly loved their lovers enough to love them. Her stories ended in wistfulness with the characters almost holding hands. Two were sold to the movies but never produced.

It occurs to me that you're probably not very interested in Miss Carol. No doubt I've made some mistakes. In my descriptions I forgot to tell you how she looked, the color of her hair or skin or eyes. I neglected to mention her bearing and/or carriage and said nothing at all about her interpersonal relations.

Wallace Stevens once said, "Description is revelation," and you know, I fell for it. If you want to know any of the nonrevelations you'll have to help me out; after all, readers and listeners are always friends.

I can only tell you that Joyce Carol is modest and desperate. She has a peasant's cunning, and you would not want to be her sister or roommate. She spends a lot of time missing her weight-lifter husband. The five offspring and the thirty-nine novels do not make her miss him any less. She sits at the word processor and imagines his strained biceps. When he pushed the bar over his head he grunted like an earthquake and won her heart.

In her own life Joyce Carol is undeluded by romantic conventions. Her stories may be formulaic but she knows that the shortness of life, the quirks of fate, the vagaries of love are always the subjects of literature.

Sometimes her word processor seems less useful than a 19-cent pen. Sometimes she feels like drowning herself in a mud puddle.

Still she is neither depressed nor morose. She is sitting there before you virtually undescribed, a schematic past, a vague future, possibly a bad credit risk as well.

Lots of times the strings of words she composes make all the difference to her. In the paragraph she has just written, a knight has survived the plague though everyone with him has perished. He carries a bag of infidel teeth as a souvenir for his lady. His horse slouches away from Bethlehem.

Joyce Carol looks up from her labor. The wet nurses are cuddling the babes. She is glad that she did not choose to bottle-feed. The *Enquirer* photographer snaps his pictures. In the photographs the fingers of the infants almost touch. Everything is the way it is.

Eskimo Love

My Eskimo love has no gaps between her teeth. Her face, barely visible beneath a sealskin parka, glows in the dark. She is crinkling her nose. She holds a fish in her left hand for the *National Geographic* photographer. From the fish she has learned the secrets of the sea. Her eyes, accustomed to long stretches of barren waste, have no trouble reaching me from the glossy page.

In the background is her lifetime—big, hard, solid chunks of experience. How could it be otherwise? Take the running out of water, the babbling from brooks, remove the stream from conversation and you'll get an idea of Eskimo life.

When you bathe, think of her straddling a wooden tub in her frigid house. Think of her garden where no tomatoes grow.

It's not surprising that you cannot surprise an Eskimo or pray next to him or make him use abstract language. The Eskimo invented silence. His microbes are the size of thumbs, his viruses carry Swiss army knives. The Eskimo divides the day only twice, into light and dark, and they are not equal partners. Two Eskimos constitute a minyan.

The magazine article says that the Eskimos are a dying people, that they are eating their infrastructure, that their sisters are becoming obsolete, that in their desperation they have begun to fish from helicopters.

This is nonsense. There will always be Eskimos. I am less sure of Iranians. When I met my wife she thought I was Iranian. The room was lit like the fourteenth century. The hum of conversation sounded like the Tower of Babel.

"Hel-lo," she said to me. "My name is VICKI. How ARE YEW?"

"I'm from Michigan," I told her.

She moved so close that even in the soupy light I could have examined her ears.

"I would have guessed Teheran. So swarthy in the Midwest? You never know."

She came to international parties looking for remnants of the Ottoman Empire—Turks, Bedouins, hill and desert people with a grudge against history.

I searched the crowd for Eskimos.

We found each other.

"I wanted a more exotic husband," she said, "someone with four or five names whose grandfather was a shepherd. Once I knew such a man, Mohammed Al-Khali. He was from the Sudan. His grandfather remembered seeing the head of General Gordon on the walls of Khartoum. We had a brief romance. English was his fourth language, French his fifth. He got them mixed up. Sometimes he 'amoured' me, sometimes he 'loaved' me. I learned how to say 'Your father is a descendant of Omar' in Arabic. He knew Parsee. His first roommate was a Zoroastrian.

"When I brought him home to meet my parents, Mother just wanted to know if he was a Negro. He wore a white burnoose so she couldn't see if his hair was kinky.

"He was a very funny man. He threw his chicken bones on the floor. Mother kept asking him if the Sudan was anything like Jamaica, where she spent her honeymoon.

" 'Call me Mo,' he said. He kissed her hand. While we were dating he sent me a velvet rug that had a picture of a girl with a mustache. He sent Mother a brass-plated samovar. We were suburban hillbillies to him.

"He said the Fourth World was the most interesting. He studied economics and went to all the X-rated movies."

"Would you like me more if I had that kind of background?"

She wrinkled her nose like the Eskimo. She laughed. She kissed me. "Maybe," she said, "who knows?"

"I wanted an Eskimo wife, a high-cheeked woman with a face framed in fur."

"Well," Vicki said, "you're dark enough for me, am I Eskimo enough for you?"

A lot of times on the edge of sleep it occurs to me that if Vicki had been an Eskimo she might have lived longer. We were married five years. We were almost ready to go traveling—north was going to be first. She bought nylon leggings and big red Mickey Mouse mittens.

"You know," my friend Oscar is telling me, "talking to you is like taking group therapy with engineers. I froze an hour ago. I have feeling only in my tongue and bladder, and you stand on the ice daydreaming. If my tear ducts were not frozen I would cry."

Oscar is my best friend. He is on the ice as an act of love. When I told him I was going ice fishing he insisted on coming along. Neither of us had ever done it. I bought a pickax and fishing line. Oscar brought along a nylon rope. He tied the rope around my waist, then moved to dry land to save me when necessary. He carried a book and some Chapstick. He expected to be bored but had no idea how cold he would get standing as lifeguard on a frozen lake.

"Please," Oscar says, "I promise if you leave now I won't bother you with social engagements for a month. I won't tell you to stop mourning. I won't advise you to be happy. I'll go to nature study or séance classes with you, anything you want, only let's get out of here."

Oscar's specialty is art. He doesn't have to chip through many inches of ten-thousand-year-old rain to find what he wants.

"All I have to do," he says, "is go to an opening at a gallery. Just put me in a room of well-dressed, intelligent women—hang even mediocre art on the walls. Provide a few drinks, some atmosphere for the heart to sing in, that's all it takes.

"There is no excitement like indoor excitement—in a gallery under a tuxedo with all the false talk in the air and money nobody has earned.

"Stop being crazy. What are we doing here on terra incognita? Why am I standing on a lake? Come, Narcissus of the North, before there's nothing left of you. Come into the warmth of art—if not art, photography. If not photography, poetry. I'll show you the books to read. Forget Eskimos. I'm sorry I came along. Friendship is not calamity."

He talks while I chip away at the ice. The dry land he stands on is distinguishable only by a clump of trees. I show my concern for him by checking the pickax to make sure that the top won't fly off to kill Oscar ten yards away under the icy branches.

"If it melts you're a goner," he says.

"This ice could only melt if the sun went skin diving right now. Gravity itself protects me. The sun knows what's up. The moon and stars too, that's why they're always in love songs."

"Oh, my obsessed friend," Oscar says, "the world and all its unhappiness can still be yours. What isn't isn't. When you break through the ice it will still be plenty cold underneath."

About this he's right. It's no Miami Beach in my six-inch hole. I thought the fish would rise to the top, the cream of the ocean bobbing up to see me bringing light to the depths.

"Let there be light," I said to the fish. And there was light. The sun burned through clouds and seasons and left other planets lonesome for an instant to spit one bright shot down the rough sides of my hole in the lake.

But no fish came to look at the glare from the sky. Oscar covered his eyes and wept.

"I can't leave you here to die, but in another hour we'll both freeze. Come to my neighborhood Safeway. Make yourself comfortable. Lie down in the freezer right next to the haddock. When they arrest you, I'll bail you out. Risk your life in taxicabs and bad neighborhoods. Give yourself a break."

I am thinking of the Eskimo, who arise before dawn and chop such holes and come home to their women sometimes empty-handed like me. The Eskimo woman does not upbraid her man. She looks at him with big round eyes.

"Our little ones," he tells her, "will have to eat dried blubber." She rubs him under his parka.

"When the ice melts," he vows, "I'll row on down to the Arctic Circle and lasso whale calves and spring shark. You'll see. We'll drink hot shark-fin soup and watch the sun never set."

What does he care about food, about cold, about hunger, about anything but the Eskimo woman?

"For you," he says. "The aurora borealis shines for you."

"I've known self-destructive people," Oscar says. "After all, who isn't a little hostile to his own bag of bones? But you are a prizewinner. For daily life you're too tired—a foreign movie, an interesting woman, that's all too hard for you. But dress up like Santa Claus and chop ice for two hours, for this you have energy. Here you are happy, talkative. In a room of civilized people you become the Eskimo."

Just before we leave, just before I put back the half circle of ice I have cut away and rub spit along the crack to forever seal my violation of the surface, just then I get a bite.

When the line tightens I tilt on the ice; even a gentle tug can pull you in when there's no good place to stand. I reach for the slippery fish but it's only Vicki. She was in the area, she got entangled in the line. Not a bite, an accident. I see her frozen lips, her fish eyes. I cut her loose. We have already had our last words. Some deaths are final.

Why is it when you cut a slot into the underworld you always find your own dead?

"Please." Oscar is begging. As he shivers, the safety rope dances around his waist like a dying insect. He is stomping his feet and embracing himself, things he must have learned you're supposed to do to keep from freezing. There are not even footprints, no record on the ice of our having been here. I roll up my line, then bend to lick the surface clean. Already the mark of my ax is disappearing in the cold.

"That's it," Oscar says, "kiss the ice, lick it, make yourself at home. Why should you jog or swim like other people, why should you go on Club Med holidays when there is all this—" He gestures with his shivering arm at Lake Michigan. "Who needs music and friends and books and movies when you've got this frozen playground?"

Oscar is a specialist in women too. Last year an art historian loved him, this year a painter. Some woman with talent and insight always manages to fall in love with him.

"It's not actually love," Oscar says, "it's just how certain people respond to a given aesthetic environment."

He has recently stopped smoking. When he talks he still pauses as if he's inhaling. It makes the talk a little jerky, sad, elegiac. Oscar is a happy man, but sadness is his calling.

"My mother was an enthusiast," he says. "She exuded. A telephone ringing made her happy; to her, gagging was a sign of life. My sisters and I moped just to get even. On school vacations we spent whole days in our rumpled bedclothes.

"At the beach where she loved to show her heavy belly in a two-piece suit, I wore dark long-sleeved shirts. I resented the fact that she made me oil her back. There I was, a nine-year-old in long sleeves rubbing Coppertone into his mother's rib cage. The cuffs of my long-sleeved shirt glistened with suntan oil."

He looks at his fingers, thinking of Marlboros. "She's dead twelve years and I'm almost middle-aged. I have sat on the French Riviera and remembered my mother glistening on the rocks near Mona Lake."

Oscar is not sentimental, but he's always about to cry. While his artistic girlfriends hold and comfort him, he criticizes their paintings.

His current partner is Madelyn, her project the color brown. We are stalking brown. In the Michigan autumn it is everywhere, but we have driven two hundred miles for Madelyn to see brown against Saginaw Bay, where the spectroscope leads her like a compass.

"I want the brown of fir trees," she says, "in October when the leaves are changing but the trunks are not."

I am here on this outing for Oscar. I owe him for the fishing. This is what friends are for. For me he shivered, for him I help Madelyn set up a tripod so she can photograph and later paint the brown that has never been.

He and Madelyn have brought along a partner for me. Not an Eskimo, but at least she has lived in Alaska. Sue, a former tour guide in a plaid flannel shirt unbuttoned three buttons. L. L. Bean shoes, teeth like lightning rods. Sue, queen-to-be of my igloo.

Her health is enough to scare me. She worked for the Sierra Club, she was a midwife, she has climbed Mt. McKinley. She is out getting firewood.

"Not many big sticks," Sue says. "There have been so many campers they've used up all the big sticks." She carries an armload of wood that would burden a donkey.

To her, big sticks must be logs the size of telephone poles. They have found me a Paul Bunyan. Oscar and I start the fire while Sue goes to seek more forests.

"You're afraid of women," Oscar says. "It's natural after what you've been through. I thought a healthy outdoor girl might be just the right kind of person for you. Take a chance," he tells me, "it doesn't have to be forever."

Madelyn is dressed in a surgical scrub suit. She is cutting the brown out of nature, sucking it into her big lens.

"Jesus," Sue tells me, coming up from behind, "this campground is like New York City."

"What do you mean?" I ask. "Traffic? Jews?"

"Just people—just so many people all over the place using up the logs, dropping Kleenex in the woods. I'm not used to it. Where I live it's walking distance to Siberia. Where I live you see someone six hours after a plane flies over you. You go weeks without talk. There is not even the noise of insects. Do you know what it's like to live on ice?"

No, only the Eskimo knows that. The photographer must have strapped her to the keel of his boat, otherwise she wouldn't stand so still holding a fish that is not even a spectacular fish. Left alone she would run away to join the girls outside the photo, the girls who are mending the nets, making the soup, carving the air with their breath. She would be one of them, laughing, working, not holding a fish aloft with the embarrassed look of a basketball player at the top of his jump who discovers that the hoop vanished as soon as he left his feet.

There must be a photograph of me holding Vicki in the air, smiling foolishly, both of us aloft.

Vicki came home, she put down her briefcase, she turned on the thermostat, she unwrapped the newspaper. She washed her face. There were little bubbles of soap still on her hairline.

She took off her pantyhose, she put on sneakers, she washed her contact lenses, she smoothed the bedspread when she stood up. She telephoned her sister, she cooked a TV dinner, she listened to a Linda Ronstadt album.

"All right," Sue says, "you know a little about ice, but the Eskimos would still surprise you. When they want to do a thing they offer no explanations. They'll get in a boat and go to Greenland for three years just to see some more snow. They think that every time they take a breath it's altogether new."

She blows her own hot breath at me.

"Your friend Madelyn," Sue says, "I'd like to burn her in her own fat."

"She has no fat, she's been on a diet all her life."

"She wouldn't last a week in the north."

Sue pitches our igloo tent. It pops up, a bright green squat dome. She puts her mackinaw inside and my sleeping bag. Sue needs no cover unless it's below 20 degrees F. In her pocket she carries a two-ounce silver emergency blanket that holds in body heat. She will never die of shock or exposure, though rescuers will be blinded by the glare of her.

"Be careful," Oscar warns me. "You've been three years without a woman. You've suffered grief. You've been a real pain in the neck to your friends. Nobody wants to listen to all that suffering. I'm glad you're better but, still, don't think you can be happy just like that.

"Watch your step. I knew you'd like that she was from Alaska. Believe me, I tried to find you a true Eskimo. I advertised in the

New York Review of Books for an intellectual Eskimo; then in the *Seattle Times* for any kind of Eskimo.

"Sue is a coincidence. I knew her old boyfriend. They were driving from Fairbanks to Alabama and had a fight in Chicago. She ended up staying with my sister-in-law. When I heard she was from Alaska I asked no questions. It seemed like destiny. Now when you get the desire for ice fishing again you can take her."

Oscar would know how to take her fishing, how to court a girl even if she was from Alaska. He would have her sifting the snow for Indian artifacts, reading the myths of seafaring peoples. She would accompany him on voyages as the painter did to southern Italy and as Helen, his folksy one, traveled to Mexico and Guatemala to collect ruins.

Oscar is the one friend I can always count on. Lots of times he just came over and sat with me. Silence is hard on him but he is capable of it.

He went with me to see Vicki. He watched me cut food into tiny morsels and then try to get her lips open. But there was no recognition, no life from Vicki, only the nurses clapping every time it looked like I might get a bit of food into her.

Oscar understood. He left me alone for a long time. He bought me an illustrated book on Eskimo life. There I read that in one of their stories the niece of God came to the new world before the *Niña,* the *Pinta,* and the *Santa Maria.* She did not like what she found. The angels had made it into a health spa and scratched their backs against the redwoods.

She returned and told everyone from Mt. Olympus to Mt. Scopus to beware of the new world. And the gods did. They stayed away by the millions, withholding counsel and wisdom and at least eight hundred years of life from every creature until the Eskimo women calmed them down with bedtime stories and fish chowder and made everything as soft and warm as a moose's thigh.

Oscar is reading an art journal. I am holding the Eskimo book. Madelyn and Sue are temporarily out of sight.

"You know," Oscar says, "there are women, and there is art, and once in a while a good meal or an important basketball game."

I tell him that we ought to go to a game soon.

"No," Oscar says, "food and basketball you can do alone and art I can't convince you about, but why don't you stop pretending you're an Eskimo or a hermit; why not rejoin mankind? You're a smart person. You can probably come up with a hundred ways to make yourself unhappy. I'm saying, play the stock market, fall in love, go to a therapist—even find a hobby. What about Save the Whale? Just stop all the brooding.

"You think I like Madelyn? You think Helen and I had such great fun in Italy? You think I live off the fat of the land? Believe me, being happy is the toughest job of all."

We drink tea and look at a small painting that Madelyn has hung from the center pole of their tent. She also dropped cut flowers next to the staking poles.

The painting is one of her own works, brown of course, the brown of a fig that has just finished being green.

"She has plenty of talent," Oscar says. "Nothing will come of it because she has no style, no sense of organization, but her eye is pure. She is the victim of a bourgeois childhood. When her mother recognized her talent they started hoping she would become a dress designer. She escaped her parents, but she doesn't know how to be free in her art."

Sue joins us in the tent. We watch Madelyn photographing brown in the last light of the day.

"I don't know much about art," Sue says, "but if you ask me, Madelyn has about as much talent as a six-year-old."

"That's it exactly," Oscar says. "Six-year-olds are pure—by ten they all become dress designers. The six-year-old is the heart of her talent. She's here just playing with color—adults don't do that."

"She's playing with a twelve-hundred-dollar camera," Sue says. "That's not what I'd call playing with color."

Madelyn pays no attention to us.

"All her talk about brown is really getting to me," Sue says, "or maybe I'm so used to talking about the weather that I don't know how to do anything else. That's about eighty percent of what we talk about in Alaska, maybe more.

"It was what started our big fight in the car on the way down. Charley kept wanting me to tune in weak stations far away so we could keep track of the weather along the route. The temperature was eighty everywhere. There were only light sprinkles and motels and rest stops what seemed every ten feet. We had lived for a year and a half in a cabin talking mostly about the weather over the shortwave. I realized somewhere around Minneapolis that Charley was going to be like this forever. A cabin in Alaska was the perfect place for his focus on one big worry. I couldn't stand it. By Chicago I hated him and got out of the car. I even gave him most of my gear. I just wanted to get away and it would have taken all day to repack. I'm carrying everything I own in my backpack."

"Well," Oscar says, "didn't I tell you this was the girl for you?"

Sue laughs. "Don't you have any possessions either?"

"Too many. I've been running from them all my life. But they catch me one by one. In Dayton, Ohio, I found my color TV and in a motel in New Hampshire I ran across the pillow of my childhood. I could go on." I did not tell her about catching Vicki under the ice.

"I get the picture," she said. "You steal from motels."

Madelyn joins us at sunset. Her project before brown was painting the underside of fingernails. Hers are cinnamon but smoky, dulled by all the dead thickness of her fingernail. Sue examines Madelyn's nails and hears about the project.

"There were a whole group of us from the Art Institute," Madelyn says. "We even copyrighted the idea. I think it would have gone over but we tried to market it just when punk was getting big, and who could compete with blue hair and safety pins?

"I thought we would change the way women did their nails forever. That would be a big thing, you know—I mean, nails don't seem like much but think about how many billions of them there are on earth. It's a pretty harmless and interesting way to change history. We were like those monks who thought the world would change if they got a certain percentage of the human population to meditate. I like to think in global terms."

"I thought you just had dirty fingernails," Sue said. "A high percentage of the human population does."

"Most of the dull people made the same joke. We went over least well at a convention for cosmetologists. Did you go to beauty school?"

"No," Sue says. "I educated myself reading the *Encyclopaedia Britannica* in the back corner of our shack."

"Enough," Oscar says. "We can taunt each other after dinner."

I watch Sue stack the logs. Madelyn places her rolls of film carefully in a brown leather bag. Oscar and I begin to assemble the meal. Madelyn puts on her gold sun visor and moves to a small hill to observe the sunset and the three of us. She is like an Egyptian overseer peering at slaves, imagining pyramids.

"Is she always this awful?" I ask Oscar.

"I'm glad you're expressing this hospitality," he says. "It's a good sign. You don't have to like her, she's my girlfriend, not yours. . . . Of course, I hate her too. It's part of the attraction."

After dinner I walk alongside the creek. Madelyn and Oscar are snug in their tent reading in the light of a Coleman lantern. Oscar even carries an extra wick; he can't sleep without thirty minutes of reading no matter what the circumstances.

Sue has gone into our igloo. She is not my Eskimo, but she is strong and young and honest. I see her figure emerge wrapped in her ultra-light silver blanket. She comes toward me across the darkness like Halley's comet.

"I don't know very much about you," she says, "and I can't stand your friends. I'm not crazy about your pop-up tent either. It seems like all of you need to be turned upside down and hung out in the sun for a while."

In the darkness I can only see her blanket. She says that she will never return to the frozen tundra, to the talk of weather, to the company of Eskimos.

"I hate to disappoint you," she tells me, "but the Eskimos are not gods. They're just like us. They take vacations—they use electric blankets . . . c'mon."

She takes my hand and pulls me into the creek. The water is no higher than my knees and surprisingly warm—warmer even than the air. The noise of our splashing doesn't bother a soul. I chase Sue through the creek. Stumbling on rocks we fall onto one another, laughing. There is no fish, no ice, no ghost underfoot, no Eskimo —just water—just camping with friends on a warm night in the middle of my life. It's enough.

The National Debt

The keeper of the National Debt is a modest man who, until recently, was never in the public eye.

"My ancestors," he says, "they were used to royalty, accustomed to attention. My great-grandfather played whist with Rothschild and wore the satins of the House of Hapsburg. The nineteenth century, that was one of the truly great times for national debts. These days, at least until recently, all the glamour was gone."

"You should have seen him," his wife says, "when NBC called to invite him to be on *Meet the Press.* He was so nervous I began to worry about how his feelings might affect the debt. Finally he canceled. They did a show on the environment instead."

The keeper and his wife live modestly. Their address is classified but it's distant from Washington and in a respectable neighborhood of a major city not far from the Sun Belt and poised between the Great Plains and the Industrial Heartland.

The keeper has no political affiliation. "My vision of the world," he says, "is obviously influenced by my closeness to the debt. It's my life, my career, my raison d'être. Other than that I'm just plain folks."

He admits to feeling defensive about his charge. "Strictly speaking, the debt is a very straightforward item, nothing to get emotional about. Still, over the years I've grown attached. I guess it's only human to do so. It irks me no end to see the debt attacked as if it's war, famine, or disease. The debt is such an easy mark that everyone has a go at it. It's a mere three percent of the national pie, a slice no larger than a dieting aunt takes on Thanksgiving Day after stuffing herself on turkey and dressing. The debt has never hurt a living soul. The biggest item in the debt is liberty. Unfortunately we can't compute it, but we do know that, adjusted to 1967 freedoms, there is less than a two-percent annualized return on totalitarianism."

The keeper has been at his work for so many years that even the unusual recent growth of the debt is no surprise to him.

"The only thing I don't like," he says, "is the public relations side of it. At first I thought it was a good idea. I helped organize the original 'Debt Roast' and 'Debt Appreciation Night.' But when they started all those debt hotlines I thought it had gone too far."

Today is a special day for the National Debt. On this day it surpasses the accumulated owing of all civilizations prior to World War II. The keeper and his wife are having a quiet glass of champagne on their front porch. No network or wire service has covered the event. The debt sits beside them like a mushroom growing under a tree. The keeper remembers when the debt was so small that Eleanor Roosevelt's hat covered it entirely. He remembers that Dwight Eisenhower never visited, that Nixon sent only John Connally to pay his respects.

"These days," his wife says, "it's easy to keep the debt. But I remember when he actually had to feed it by hand and carry out all the calculations." She sighs. "My husband was a strong young man then. He had to be; the debt was mighty frisky."

"Yes," the keeper says, "I did it all by hand but I was never afraid. In my family they always talked about the Hapsburg debt. Debt is as American to me as baseball. In my opinion people worry too much about the debt. Believe me, the debt is in good hands. If I was people, I would still worry about teenage gangs and drugs and the lack of moral values and when to change your oil and what school to send the children to and whether your team is in the pennant race. I wouldn't worry about the debt."

"That's easy for you to say," his wife says. She rises from her wicker chair. "You understand the debt. Everyone else thinks about interest."

"Interest," says the keeper. "I have no interest in interest. It's as separate from the debt as dental floss is from athlete's foot powder. Besides, the interest keepers are not our kind of people."

The debt purrs like a kitten beside him.

"The interest people are just electricians. They monkey around with computers that could figure out the origins of species in three seconds. They're whiz kids at math, or politicians, or phenomenologists. They don't have the spirit of keepers, and most of them don't even understand that the very essence of debt is constancy. Socrates, the wisest man, understood debt. His last words were, 'I owe a cock to Aesculapius.'

"I know that when I'm gone they'll treat it differently—maybe they'll incorporate it. Who knows? Congress in one fell swoop might even abolish it."

"God forbid," says his wife.

"Who knows?" the keeper says. "For thirty-eight years I've been doing this day by day. Everyone talks about leaving the debt to future generations, but sometimes I wonder if they'll even appreciate it. Sometimes I think they ought to be left to create their own debt.

"As far as I'm concerned, I wouldn't want to live in a nation that had no debt. My wife and I raised our own children to be borrowers and lenders.

"The whole of the debt takes up less than thirty percent of the living space of our house and it's dependable and easy to service and sleeps through the night. This debt, this very private quiet misunderstood thing, is not your enemy. I just wish people would forget about it and go back to worrying about scarce resources. You can talk forever about coal and oil and uranium, but the debt"— he looks at his wife, content on the porch beside him—"the debt is just a part of us."

"Debt thou art," she says, "to debt thou shalt return."

The elderly couple hold one another's hands. The sun shines. Children across the street play freeze tag. Inside, quietly, constantly, peacefully, the debt mounts.

The Four Apples

J essica popped out of Debby's tummy and said, "Tell me a story, Dad." While a nurse wiped the other world from her eyes I started to tell. All the kids from my own childhood appeared. There was Bad Bernie throwing stones at people, Marky Fixler riding his purple bike, and his little brother Gonzalez trying to pedal a scooter alongside him. My sisters were there too, dressing me up in their old clothes and pushing me around in a buggy. The stories made so much noise that the doctor told us to leave the hospital.

But the stories followed us home. They filled up the playpen and the yard. When Jessica ate she mixed them with baby food and smeared her face and laughed. She threw the rubber-coated spoon at me and yelled, "More stories!"

So I told her about my grandma, and the Grandma stories brought in people with beards and funny clothes from Europe, people who were bakers and farmers and fishermen. And they made us feel lazy for not working as hard as they did. The new stories took up so much room that we had to move to a bigger house. Then, when all the stories and Jessica and Debby and I got comfortable in our new house, just then Sam popped out of Debby's tummy and said, "Tell me a story, my own story not Jessica's, and make it about garbage and tell it right this minute."

So for Sam all the witches and monsters and heroes that I knew came to our house and they all made noises like the garbage truck and they all thought it was fine to crawl around without a diaper. All the witches and monsters and heroes liked to get together with Sam and Jessica to play water city. They turned the kitchen floor into the ocean so they could swim between the refrigerator and the stove. But when Sam got to be two he said, "Enough baby stuff." He took out a long straw and sucked water city clean. He bought himself a TV with an antenna that reached the moon. He and Jessica found an old convertible and hired Mr. Rogers to drive it. They tied me to the back seat with spaghetti and fed me cheese sandwiches and beer as long as I kept telling them stories. When I complained, they pulled out the radio and stuck me into the dashboard.

Debby said, "Enough stories, let them go to bed." Even Mr. Rogers got tired of driving so he swallowed the car and hid in the TV. Jessica and Sam hated bedtime until they discovered the secret of the thumb. Now they know that if they suck their thumb and curl their hair the stories will keep right on all night unless they have to stop for some water or apple juice. During the night the stories crawl on the walls and hang from the ceiling. In the daytime they make yucky food good. You can squeeze them into a lunchbox or let them get big and take over the whole playground. They're faster than running shoes.

When Jessica and Sam wake up, they put on clean clothes and push the old stories out the door. There George the dog licks and smells them before he sends them down the street to Sally or Ilana, who are always sending us their stories too.

At nursery school the kids trade stories like stocks and bonds. Jessica grows rich and corners the market. She hires Sam to protect her wealth. He stuffs a water pistol into his training pants. She and her staff of girls circle the playground, gossiping, practicing numbers. They hold hands and are quiet around the boys. The stories pile up like snow. They fill the school too. Finally, when Jessica learns to read she files the stories into books where they fit just right. "It's a miracle," she tells Sam, but he's still suspicious. He saw three capital R's running down the page and had to squirt them. It's his job to tear out some of the pages and turn them upside down. He is very good at his work. Jessica tapes the words back in place.

Now that most of the stories behave and stay in the books, we have lots of room in the house. I tell only five new ones at bedtime. The kids suck their thumbs and turn those five into a hundred.

Debby comes home from work. She tells me her stories. I suck my pen and turn hers into new ones. Sam and Jessica roll off the mattress, George barks at the wind, the stories bounce off the walls.

Help

nflation is killing us, and to top it off three Mexican maids have refused to live in our house. Al says he doesn't understand how illegal aliens can be so fussy. The house is reasonable and the kids aren't hyperactive.

"All a maid will have to do," he says, "is break up fights and make peanut butter sandwiches. We've already got a Phonemate."

"Do you think that's all I do?" I ask him. "Break up fights and make sandwiches?"

"Let's not start this one," he says. "It's 1979, we've already had our confrontations."

I know what he means. He's right. If we could just find a damn maid I'd go to work tomorrow.

Al knows a little Spanish, I don't have any. Irene, my friend who was a Spanish major at UT, does all our calling. She drives a Mercedes and is accustomed to live-in help. I'm sure Irene has no sympathy for me, she just likes to practice her Spanish. She calls a man named Lopez, some kind of security guard who apparently knows lots of girls who sneak across the border. This Lopez calls me in bad English at midnight when his shift is over.

"I got nice girls from Tampico," he says, "from Oaxaca too, girls from good family, very intelligent, good companies."

"I don't want a bride," I tell him, "just a maid."

"Oh, very fine maids, do everything."

I imagine him in a phone booth curling the greasy tips of his mustache, a regular Mexican bandido, a slave trader. What does that make me?

"There's something in it for you, Lopez."

"*Sí,*" he says, "but Lopez just like to help out."

Lopez calls three times but never sends any of his girls. "Probably," I tell Irene, "he got better prices from white slavers."

"You're too sensitive," she says. "You're going about it all wrong. You're buying a service, not a person. It's like going to the beauty shop."

After months of seeking, Consuela comes, recommended by a friend of Linda's maid, Maria. On the day she arrives both kids have just recovered from chicken pox. I'm desperate enough to hire a fascist. Al has been gone for two weeks on business, and I've been alone to entertain my poxed children. I wish I'd catch it too so all three of us could check into a nursing home.

Consuela speaks no English. Her right eye is totally crossed. It's so bad it makes me gag just to look at it. She carries all her belongings in a paper bag. Maria is with her. "She work at least seex month," Maria says. "Must promise seex month or no stay here."

"I promise," I say. Maybe Lopez was right to describe them as brides. Jill and Jeremy say she's ugly. She smiles and from her paper bag brings forth shorts and a sleeveless shirt. I show her to her room. In ten minutes she's dusting fake antiques.

Irene comes over to check her. "They've never seen a regular doctor, I'd get her a chest X-ray just to be safe. She'll be handling food."

Her first night she handles the vegetables I would have thrown out and salvages the good parts to make a big crisp salad.

Al munches happily on his brownish lettuce. "This is how to fight inflation," he says, "a little at a time."

On Monday I start work.

II

Couples come to a real estate office to hate each other in front of a stranger. Husband and wife have no mutual tastes. Some of the men pretend they would as soon have an outhouse as a wallpapered bathroom. I toss my business card and a ballpoint pen at everyone, but none of them remember my name. I wear tailored dresses and carry the lockbox key. I feel like a well-groomed jailer.

Jane, who shares a desk with me, made the million-dollar sales club last year. "It takes persistence," she says, "and you have to like to drive. Who takes care of your children?"

"A cross-eyed girl who speaks no English and never had a chest X-ray." My own words scare me. I rush home to check on Jill and Jeremy. An old pickup truck is backing out of my driveway. I run in screaming for the children. They're both asleep and startled by my screams. Consuela's hair is a little messy. She's wearing lipstick.

"Who was here in a truck?" I ask.

She smiles and turns on the vacuum cleaner. My jewelry box is intact, and the color TV and the stereo are fine. I'm depressed when I realize that these are my only valuable possessions. "Ten years of marriage," I tell Al, "and besides the kids and the car we have a one-carat diamond, a TV, and a stereo."

"What about the house?" he says.

"All right," I say, "if a thirty-year mortgage counts."

"What's the big deal?" he says. "So she has a boyfriend in a pickup truck who doesn't steal. We should be happy for her. With that eye you wouldn't think she'd have a boyfriend."

She's right there while we talk, in the kitchen making tortillas, refried beans and Spanish rice.

"Looking at her eye makes me sick," I say. "Can't we do something?"

"You're upset," Al says, "because she's replacing you in the household. It's elementary psychology."

"Did you read a *Time* essay on that?"

He takes the kids for a walk and slams the door on the way out.

I try to help her in the kitchen. "Do you have any pain?" I ask. I go to the Spanish dictionary. *"Dolor,"* I say, "pain." She nods, goes to her room, and comes out with a cracking vinyl purse. She takes out six dollar bills and offers them to me.

When Al and the kids come back I'm crying in my room.

The pickup, I learn over the next few weeks, belongs to Luis. The kids tell me this. Jill says Luis has a long mustache and curly hair. I think he must be Lopez, the security guard, and I suspect some kind of conspiracy but Al tells me to calm down and concentrate on real estate. "When your own career is established," he says, "you won't worry so much about what is going on behind your back at your home."

"How can I not worry about the children?"

"Luis," he says, "is not having relations with your children."

"But he probably is with Consuela."

"That's their business."

"In my house it's my business."

Al shrugs his shoulders, then refuses to tell her that Luis can't come into the house.

Irene agrees to deliver the message. "Of course she shouldn't be having boyfriends in your house. Anyone else would throw her out in a minute. You two are naive because you've never had a live-in before."

"But what if she just goes outside to the pickup and ignores Jill and Jeremy?"

"I'll tell her no boyfriend period, not at work. What she does on weekends is her own business."

Consuela sulks after Irene delivers the message. I think I'm secretly hoping that she'll pack her paper bag and take her crossed eyes out of my life. But she stays. Every day I quiz the children about the appearance of men, Luis or others. They say there are none. Consuela's English isn't good enough to convince the children of anything, so I know that it's true. I've succeeded in interrupting the romance of a lonely cross-eyed alien.

"Stop it," Al says, "just stop it. I'm sick of hearing about Consuela: 'Consuela's eye, Consuela's boyfriend, Consuela's tortillas.' When I come home from work I want to hear about my wife and children. And I'm going to tell her to shut off that Mexican radio station when I'm home. Those marimbas are driving me crazy."

When the dinner dishes are done and Al has settled down to fall asleep over the sports page I feel like we're in the nineteenth century. Consuela sits with the children and does needlepoint. She made a little kit for Jill, who imitates her, and Jeremy uses one of those toy sewing kits with a big blunt needle. Consuela sings or hums and the children work happily until bedtime. They do this in front of the fireplace that Consuela faithfully lights each night, even though it's rarely cold enough to need it. Consuela herself is embroidering an elaborate pillow cover. On it are several human figures, some goats, and some trees and flowers. It looks like months of work. I can hardly believe that the children are doing this instead of watching TV.

When I express my admiration to Irene she says it's peasant virtue that I admire. "I went through that stage too," she says, "with one of our maids. It got so that I would stay home with her, polishing silver and singing Spanish folk songs. I felt like I was in a light opera all day. It lasted about a week. It may look peaceful, but peasant life is very, very dull."

At the office, Jane laughs when I try to crochet between property calls. "What are you going to do," she says, "embroider *Home Sweet Home* every time you sell a house?"

"I'm just sick of everything being so contemporary," I tell her. "Every house I show has four digital clocks." While we talk, the computer in the back room is typing out every new listing in the city. The words "charming" and "rustic" appear on the computer as often as "the" or "and." I feel charming and rustic myself as I crochet in our shopping center office.

Jane answers a call about my own house. It's Jill. "Luis is here," my six-year-old says. "I told you I'd tell."

Ah, my sweet child, would you call the immigration authorities too. The Gestapo? I have trained you better than Consuela has. I consider calling Irene, but I realize that the responsibility is mine alone. I put down my crocheting and pull on my new Calvin Klein suede jacket. If I had a whip I would probably take it along to make me feel more like a master.

On the drive home I imagine Consuela and Luis embracing. She will be dressed in my lingerie. Luis is all rough and still smelly from his work as a gardener or trash collector. My children listen at the door, positioning their Montessori toys with maximum efficiency. I know that Consuela lets them drink Coke and eat candy even though I've left instructions against it. I rehearse my indignant speech even though I know neither Consuela nor Luis will understand it. Here they are, creatures of the senses acting out their simple destiny, until I, a licensed realtor, swoop down upon them.

"I've given you a good home," I'll tell her, "and pay you the minimum wage even though I don't have to. You have weekends off and I help with the dishes every night. You have a portable TV in your room and the *Reader's Digest* in Spanish. I don't care if you talk on the phone all day and only vacuum once a week. Just watch my children and keep your lover away from my house. Is that asking too much?"

"Yes," she will answer, "I work as hard as you do. Is it my fault that destiny is cruel, that I was born a few hundred miles south of you in a country of no opportunity? How would you like to watch my children while I sell haciendas?"

My hands tremble on the steering wheel as I wonder how I would answer the charges she might make against me if she spoke English and dared to confront me as I am now going to confront her.

The rusting pickup with wooden sides is in my driveway. I park on the street so that I won't block him in. I wouldn't be more nervous if I was expecting to find Al with another woman.

The children are playing Candyland in their room. Consuela's lipstick is smeared. At my dinette is Luis drinking iced tea and smoking a Viceroy. He stands when I come in and bows in the European manner. He wears a digital watch and a nice khaki work suit.

Consuela's bad eye leaks a tear that has to climb the bridge of her nose before it can run down her cheek.

"I understand your rules, ma'am," Luis says in very good English.

"Please don't be angry at Consuela, the fault is entirely my own."
He offers me his business card: *Luis Rodriguez—Landscape Design.* "It
is my hope that you can use my services here and perhaps at some
of the homes you sell."

He gives me a ballpoint pen with his name and phone number.

"Your azaleas, ma'am, need some regular upkeep and your ferns
are very very dry. If you'd like I can give you an estimate for weekly
care. It would include rebedding and peat moss. My rates," he adds,
"are most reasonable."

Consuela goes to wet-mop the hallways. The kids run in for some
popcorn and are surprised to find me at home. I reach into my purse
and give Luis my card and ballpoint pen. "Perhaps you know some
Spanish-speaking couples in the market for a home," I say.

Luis nods his head. "Inflation is making it difficult," he says, "but
I will keep my eyes open." We shake hands. Professionals understand each other.

Kitty Partners

■▰■▰■▰

Simmons lives outside the odds. He goes for an inside straight the way other people order a hamburger. About once a week he hits a royal flush. Nobody bets into his check. He throws away two pair and thinks three of a kind is a bluff. In high-low you can't read his hand and he usually goes both ways. To be his kitty partner is to get Social Security young without being disabled.

But everything else is not so easy. When Simmons leaves the poker table the odds catch up. He slams his dealing hand in the car door and the fingernails ooze blood and drop like dead flowers. His wife takes a lover and longs for socialism. His children are grade school ne'er-do-wells.

"How," I ask him, "can luck be so crazy?" He shuffles the cards one-handed, puffs on a cigar, and cries while we watch an NBA doubleheader on Sunday afternoon. To top it off he is a Knicks fan. He takes the Knicks and the points but never bets them when they're favorites. What he loses on the basketball alone could buy him a Betamax recorder every year.

He squeezes a Lite beer with his good hand. I wipe the tears from his eyes with the Kleenex his kids have left on the floor.

"I'm getting out," he says. "I'm up to here. No more poker—just a regular job, a decent life."

"Like mine," I say, "kissing ass all day to sell a few copying machines. My life starts when we get to the games at night."

"Mort," he says, "you've been my kitty partner for three years. I don't want to leave you stranded."

To me he's like an oil well—I get three or four thousand a year for my 10 percent of him. On my own I play about even and can only afford the big games because of Simmons.

He cries into his beer. "I want eight hours of steady work and a little friendship during the day, a little no-suspense, a little no-bluffing. I would like to be useful with my hands: auto mechanics, maybe, or electricity. I could go to a trade school. It's not too late."

His wife, I know, has been screwing the carpenter who is remodeling the kitchen. When we come in for a drink after a game at one or two in the morning you can see a trail of nails and sawdust from the kitchen to the bedroom. She ignores the kids and tells Simmons that her beauty fades by the hour. She stands in front of a mirror naked and weighs herself on a digital scale. I've seen it myself. None of them close doors.

"Her life is hard," he says. "What woman wants to be known as a gambler's wife?"

I keep my mouth shut. Who knows what happens between man and wife? I step over the nails and go home. If I had the choice I'd take his poker luck and all his troubles.

One night we are in a ten-twenty game with six lawyers. They're all buddies from one of the big firms and have heard about Simmons. Each lawyer thinks he's a real cardsharp. I'm there as a kind of extra. After I drop three hundred I sit out the evening and watch my kitty partner. If we're lucky, my 10 percent of him will bring me back to even. The six lawyers talk like they run the country. We're playing in the house of one who has an autographed picture of Gerald Ford. They are talking about calling the Energy Department about this and someone in France or Turkey about that. They sound loose and easy, but they count and memorize every card as it leaves the deck. They wear suede vests and Gucci loafers. Simmons already looks like an auto mechanic among them. He keeps quiet and holds his bad hand in his lap.

They tease him about playing with himself. "He rubs his nuts for luck," one of the lawyers says. "When it gets hard he raises." They laugh. Simmons does raise into what must be a six-hundred-dollar pot, and four of the lawyers call. Who can blame them? He has nothing showing but explodes a pair of kings and a nine for a full house. The lawyers shake their heads and buy more chips.

After the game they huddle like a football team and offer to bankroll him in Las Vegas. "We heard you were the best," they say. "Why not go for the really big money? You're throwing yourself away in ten-dollar games. We'll back you, fifty-fifty."

I keep my mouth shut. I don't want to lose him, but maybe he'll take me along like a rabbit's foot. I could get a leave of absence from IBM. If it worked out, I'd quit and try to salvage a little something from the pension fund.

Simmons says he'll think about it.

She's still up when we get to his house. There are no nails on the carpet. She is wearing a bra and panties and doing bent-knee sit-ups. Sweat rolls down her cheeks and her face is pink. She pays no attention to me. He bends down to kiss her and I can almost taste the salt on her lips from way across the room. She finishes a set of about fifty sit-ups and covers her crotch with a *Sports Illustrated.*

He likes an icepack on his head after a long game. I go to make one up. When I come back she is wearing a robe and sitting on his lap. They may already be doing it. I put the ice on his head and leave.

She nixes Vegas. "He'd find another woman in two days out there," she tells me. "In that town women are like sand. I can't take the sun, either, and my hair would go limp. The kids don't want to leave their friends and after all there's no security." She says all this knowing he is unbeatable at poker.

Simmons enrolls in a once-a-week class in auto mechanics. It breaks my heart because I know we're missing a good game but I drive him there. He has a license but didn't learn to drive until he was almost twenty-six. He only does it when he has to. She hates the car too. They both grew up in New York riding the subways. They have a '78 LTD that needs a new battery every few months because the kids play with it in the garage and leave the lights on. I'm the only one who gets aggravated about it.

The kids, Jan and Joan, are not twins but they might as well be. One is a boy and the other a girl and they're two years apart but they're the same size and both have dirty-blond hair. They're always asking for nickels. She taught the boy to roll cigarettes. Nobody smokes, it's just a little hobby. He's only six but can roll them tight as a Lucky Strike. Now and then I bring him a few packs of Ojibwa papers. He usually has little strands of loose tobacco hanging from a corner of his mouth. He says he wishes he belonged to people that smoked. Both of them call me "Uncle Mort."

Simmons soaks in the tub an hour before each game. They've got a stereo system that pipes into the bathroom. He prefers classical most of the time, but tonight I hear a little 1940s swing.

"I'm worried about Simmons," she says to me. She's wearing a skimpy T-shirt and tight white shorts that show the line of her underwear. She's twenty-eight, maybe thirty, and has a blondish Afro and blue eyes.

"He has no sense of satisfaction from his work. Nobody can be happy without that."

She leads me into the kitchen, a mess of Play-Doh, dirty dishes, and sawdust. "The man who is building these cupboards gets more pleasure from a smooth piece of wood than Simmons does from a thousand-dollar pot."

"I don't know about that," I say. "I've seen him pretty happy with a hundred-dollar pot."

"You don't understand," she says. "Poker is no mystery to him."

He comes downstairs all pink from the tub. He's wearing a one-piece coverall that says *Jack* in script above his heart. Nobody calls him Jack.

In the car he stretches out the best he can in the back seat.

"I don't know," he says. "I earned almost forty thousand dollars last year playing cards. I do it four or five hours. Why isn't it a regular night job like a security guard or something?"

I just drive. A lot of our games are in the far suburbs where the executives live. Simmons could play in two games a night if he wanted. He's invited everywhere. The rich men like to say they've played against him. It's worth a few hundred dollars to them. He's also very polite and nice company. A lot of people expect a professional gambler to be a kind of criminal. I did too.

I met him, just after they moved to Texas, at a $2 game in West University. It was real small potatoes, and you could see that he was embarrassed to be winning most of the money. They were all neighbors; only he and I were strangers. They each had a kitty partner. He asked me if I wanted to kitty. I'd have been crazy to say no, and it's stayed that way ever since. We each put 20 percent of every winning pot aside and split whatever is left at the end. In the game we bet into each other like enemies. We have to or it wouldn't be fair.

"I'm thinking, Mort," he says, "about going back East and maybe opening some kind of small shop: hardware, books, something that is a turnkey operation. I could supervise my business and maybe still play poker a couple of nights a week."

He sits up in the back seat and blocks my rearview mirror.

"People tell me to move to Alaska and play the pipeline workers, move to London or Saudi Arabia to play the oil sheikhs, or to Hollywood for the movie stars. I don't know." He raises his arms in despair. That night he wins $600 and is so bored he almost falls asleep.

II

When his wife leaves him, Simmons moves to a one-room apartment on the Main Street busline right across from a twenty-four-hour cafeteria. She gets the house. Neither of them wants the car.

"I could make it hard on her," he says. "I could just play in small games and have no money for child support. But why should I hurt my own children?" He takes the separation pretty well. Then, in the middle of a big hand, he closes with a pair of queens showing. It's his bet and he closes. Everyone at the table nearly pisses in his pants. Simmons goes outside for a short walk. I'm so surprised that I don't know what to say to the others. He returns and wins the next six hands. But after that it becomes a pretty regular thing. Either he closes when he's high or fails to call a small raise at the seventh card, or in high-low, where he's like a master diamond cutter, he goes the wrong way and loses everything. It doesn't hurt his income much, but it makes me wonder. He won't talk about it. "Everybody's human," he says. "I make mistakes."

His wife gets a job as a teaching assistant at the school for the deaf. She and the children learn sign language. The kids give him a book on it and he practices. They all seem to get a big kick out of it.

I've talked to her now and then since they split. When it first happened she called me.

"Take care of him, Mort," she says. "I can't live off luck anymore. It's a world of mortar and brick. Living with him is like playing double solitaire."

He knows that the carpenter has moved in with her. "Jesus Christ," I say. "You work with your hands too, and your mind and your willpower. Why the hell do you let her make you feel so guilty? Poker is real work. Ballplayers don't feel guilty about making a living, or actors who only memorize a few lines. Nobody in his right mind thinks there's anything wrong with what you do."

He shakes his head. "Mort," he says, "she married an idealist. I daydreamed about feeding the hungry, changing the world; we were both signed up for the Peace Corps. When Nixon bombed Cambodia we quit in protest. Now look at me. Some idealist. A reader of numbers.

"You know, Mort," he says, "maybe some of the people we play with really need their money. Maybe I'm hurting them."

Here he is supporting her and the carpenter and the cigarette roller and who knows how many deaf kids while he sleeps in a $90 a month room and watches a rented TV. But you can't tell him anything. If you could he'd be a happy man.

I just let him go on about injustice everywhere. It's all right when it's only the two of us, but pretty soon he starts up during games. When someone seems to be losing a lot, Simmons will take him into the next room and quietly offer to give him back his money. He's playing $20 or sometimes $50 limit with people a hundred times richer than he is. He just embarrasses them. Some of them must think he's cheating.

One day he says, "Mort, I'm starting a second kitty, twenty percent to UNICEF." He carries a Dutch Masters cigar box to the games and puts the UNICEF money in it. That plus the child support has to be hurting him. The other players think the UNICEF box is a joke, but I take him to the bank to write out the money orders.

Days he stays home reading books. I guess he sees the kids quite a bit because he says he's getting good at sign language. The kids have a charge account with Yellow Cab. He arranged it. Anytime they want to see him they just call a cab. A lot of the drivers know them by now. Sometimes I pick them up when I'm in the neighborhood after school. The carpenter is doing a good job on the house. He's put brick flower boxes all around and screened in the porch. Maybe he's done even more inside.

I see her sometimes out in front with the kids or putting out the trash. She looks even better than the house. Only Simmons suffers.

Finally, he starts to play badly. I can see what he's thinking. He's thinking that if he loses at poker then everything else will turn better for him. I tell him that I know what he's doing and that it's crazy. "All that will happen is that you'll be poor and miserable instead of fairly comfortable and miserable." He says he's not doing it on purpose.

"It's by accident that you call an open two pair when you have seven strangers, jack high?"

"Psychology," he says. "I want my adversaries to think I'm weak in the mind."

"You're convincing your friends."

He tells me I'm too materialistic. "The reason I win," he says, "is that I don't care. Detachment is the secret of poker. When what you want is the space between the numbers, it's no big deal to hit the numbers."

To me this is gibberish. "You've got a knack. Some people can cook or draw or shoot pool. A knack, that's all it is. If you don't waste it, it will make you a nice living."

"You know," he says, "there is nothing less intelligent than a computer. All it can decide is yes or no. If it weren't for speed, the computer would be less useful than the wooden shoe."

He moves out of the apartment into the YMCA, which is close by and also has a twenty-four-hour cafeteria. "Everything goes in stages," he says. "Now I have to simplify. Here I don't even own my sheets." His single luxury is the rented TV, and it's a twelve-inch black-and-white. His room is so gloomy that I stop watching ball games with him. He never goes to my apartment or anywhere else outside of the poker games. I think he's in the middle of a nervous breakdown. My instinct is to wait it out, but finally I call her and tell her what's up.

"We're all suffering," she says. "Sid lost two thirds of his ring finger on a bandsaw. The children both have viral pneumonia."

"He never comes out of that room," I tell her. "The man hasn't seen daylight in weeks. I can't stand to watch it."

"Everyone chooses his own life."

"That's not true and you know it."

"I'm too tired to argue." She hangs up.

Simmons continues to lose. For him, winning less than two or three times what the next best player takes home used to be a bad night. Suddenly he has to struggle to break even. He still gets the cards, but other people do too. It's like there's two patron saints at the table and his is weaker.

For a while I still think he's faking it, working some private deal with superstition, but when I see how sweaty his hands are and how really jumpy he is I begin to believe that it's nothing he can control.

He tells me that Orlindreyev, a famous Russian poker player in the 1890s, used to stand on his head an hour a day when he started to lose. I don't know where Simmons is getting this kind of information but I see that he is studying his problem.

"Did it help him?"

"No," he says. "Oh, he won some but a friend shot him in a duel."

It's pretty bad hearing this kind of thing in a YMCA room from a man who hasn't had a winning night in weeks. I suggest a change of scene, a vacation maybe. I know someone who has a beach house in Galveston. He says no, but Friday, after work, I literally pull him out of his room. He has no suitcase or razor, just a tan sport shirt and slacks. I lock him in the car and threaten to speed and switch lanes.

"All right, I'll go," he says. "Just take it easy on the accelerator."

At the beach he walks in the surf and sits in the sun for longer than I can take it. I cook us steaks in the backyard barbecue pit and we watch ball games on the TV. It's a perfect weekend, and I'm proud of myself for getting him out of that grimy room.

Back in Houston, his luck stays bad. I actually see him lose with four sixes. A bad player, a yokel from Austin that we see every three or four months, has pulled an inside straight flush. The pot is not too big, but it's the first time anybody there ever saw someone lose with four of a kind. It's an omen. Simmons takes it pretty well.

"I knew you had it," he says to the yokel, "but I couldn't close with four sixes."

"I guess not," the yokel says, almost choking on his good luck.

A weekend player would quit then—he'd just say so long to his buddies and stay home with the kids or take in some movies. But when you're in the Y and the game is your livelihood it's not so easy to retire.

"You're sorry now that you stopped driving me to those auto mechanics classes, aren't you."

He's right. I'm sorry.

"The game isn't over," I say. "You're only thirty-five."

"I think," he says, "that at a certain age you just don't come back. When my fingernails dropped off, the new ones grew in purplish." That night he refuses to play.

"You go ahead, Mort. I've decided."

I know he's going to kill himself. I remind him of his kids, Joanie and the cigarette roller. I tell him (it's true) that I have $11,000 put aside of kitty money, and it's all his. I'll stake him to a new career.

He hugs me and says that the kitty has been the single constant of his life. "It's a gambler's life insurance," he says. I search the room for guns, knives, even a piece of rope. He's only on the third floor and there's no poison in the bathroom.

"It's safe to leave," he says. "I've got plans." He hugs me again and thanks me for the offer of the kitty money. "I may take you up on it." This encourages me enough to leave him, but I stay outside parked across the street so I can keep my eye on his room.

In about half an hour a cab pulls up and takes him to his house. I follow the cab thinking I should call the police. Somehow he's going to kill her too, maybe all of them.

I creep up to the window carrying an emergency flashlight from my glove compartment. It's my only weapon. If I have to, I'll hit him on the head with it.

She who never closes doors has pulled the window shades. I listen at the door; then, finally thinking it might already be too late, I burst into the living room.

He is in a chair, his feet on the footstool. The children are playing with his ears.

She wears a long blue hostess gown. Her hair is straight now and at her shoulders. She has dangling earrings and looks like the Queen of Hearts. The house has painted hardwood floors and is loaded with Scandinavian lamps. There are plate-glass windows and a fireplace that must be new. The carpenter comes through the louvered doors to the kitchen carrying a tray of drinks.

"Hi," he says to me.

I stand there like a statue.

"Mort has helped me through difficulty," Simmons says. "He's a true friend."

She comes over and kisses me on the forehead. "I knew we could count on you," she says. "Thanks. Not everyone can understand fortune."

An Offering

20,000 CLASS B UNITS

MAX APPLE, INC., A PROFESSIONAL CORPORATION
(The Company)

PRICE TO PUBLIC—$100 per unit

Prior to this offering there has been no market for Max Apple, Inc., P.C. The offering price of $100 per unit has been arbitrarily determined, and there can be no assurance that a significant trading market will develop after this offering.

The underwriter, Max Apple and Max Apple, a partnership, bears no relationship to the assets, book value, net worth, net income, or other recognized criteria of value pertaining to the company.

Selected Financial Information (unaudited)

	1982	1983
Revenues	$16,053	$33,000
Net income	$16,053	$33,000
Total liabilities*	0	0

Use of proceeds: To expand Max Apple, Inc., P.C., for purchase of raw materials, for research and self-development, for general corporate purposes including working capital and pocket money.

THE COMPANY

Max Apple, Inc., P.C., is a decent, intelligent, hardworking, sometimes gloomy company, who has finally arrived at the mature stage of his development.

Formed in 1941, the result of the merger of Betty Goodstein, a teenager, and Samuel Apple, a limited partnership, the Company began his corporate career as a group of cells which was the progeny of a single cell.

His early corporate career, a generation of research and development, produced no profits. After the conclusion of his research and development phase, the Company found the political climate of the 1960s unsuitable for fiduciary concerns. The Company, on the brink of Chapter 11 proceedings, in December of 1972 found himself changing clothes in the men's room of the Palmer House Hotel in Chicago. He entered wearing blue jeans and a T-shirt bearing a silhouette of Mao Tse-tung. He emerged in a gray vested suit and appeared before a committee of Rice University, a private nonprofit institution near the Gulf Coast. Several months later the Company entered into an employment agreement with Rice University. Since that time his balance sheet has remained a constant fraction of M1.

Under terms specified in the Rice University agreement, the Com-

*There are debts resulting from a one-time special situation, marriage. However, attorneys for the corporation expect that the results of this litigation will have no substantial bearing on the proposed offering.

pany continued to create literary manuscripts in spite of the depressed academic markets. The Company produced a dissertation on Melancholy which to date has sold two microfiche copies since its initial film production in 1973 under the auspices of the University of Michigan.

BUSINESS

General development of business: On or about 1972, the Company realized that his private fantasies (See memory—Dilution, et al.) represented a marketable commodity. The Company resolved to sell his product in its initial condition rather than offering it for resale in a less intense but more familiar formula.

In the first year of operation, the Company's entire output was sold to one customer. In 1974, the Company determined to diversify his customer base and to establish himself as a reliable supplier of stories, novels, and essays fit for mass consumption. The Company adopted his slogan, "It's Only Words."

Simultaneous with the decision to expand the product line and customer base, the Company entered into a marketing agreement with the International Famous Agency of New York, N.Y., and wholesale distributors outside of the United States.

DEFINITIONS

Fiction   An event or series of events, composed of words or phrases that depict no known event or series of events composed of words or phrases.

Literature The end products of an electrochemical process, the bonding of words to a page and the subsequent use of those pages by three or more persons in a taxable manner.

Tone   A serum produced by a human or animal which has the capacity to increase the spiritual substance of a participating investor.

Reader	A being who bears no resemblance to any person living or dead.
Profit	An event which affects the immune system, thereby preventing the smooth functioning of human organisms.
Fractionation	The separation of blood from profit.
Risk	What the rich and fortunate do not understand.

MANUFACTURING

The Company manufactures its products in a suburb of Houston, Texas, in an 1800-square-foot one-floor facility. Approximately 1400 square feet are devoted to administration, 400 square feet to production.

CONSULTANTS

From time to time the Company consults the following:

1. Dr. Michael X: Dr. X, a psychoanalyst, refuses comment. The Company constantly rails against Dr. X. Dr. X's value to the Company is impossible to specify. Dr. X is a paid consultant. He receives 15 percent of the Company's gross revenues.
2. Dr. H. Huang: Dr. Huang, a naturalized citizen, is an experienced physicist who jogs with the Company. Dr. Huang's ability to approach literary material in a very direct manner is of great benefit to the Company. When presented with a work of fiction Dr. Huang asks (*a*) "What it about?" and (*b*) "It bullshit?"

Dr. Huang specifically reminds the Company that (*a*) not much has happened since the first millisecond after the Big Bang and (*b*) what is true is true only in this universe.

Dr. Huang is an unpaid consultant, though he holds an option to purchase 1,000 units of this offering at $4.95 per unit.

RISK

Risk is what you have in your hands right now. Risk is the Company's understanding that at this moment you would rather be examining an offering from a Roth, a Mailer, a Styron, or any other sure thing.

Risk is what the Company took twenty years ago to avoid becoming just like you, a lawyer or businessman with a Mercedes-Benz and a fine home looking for a quick write-off.

The Company invites you to stick your ear against its corporate chest. Go ahead. See the three gray hairs, the skin already going soft and loose. If you prefer a more scientific opinion, the Company offers itself for examination by your physician or your insurance adviser. Let someone more professional look over the goods to decide on the possibilities of a long-term investment.

The Company constantly risks lapsing into journalism or screen writing or silence.

The Company risks all by addressing you, investor; you, reader of the *Wall Street Journal;* you, taker of vacations to Europe; you, reader of best sellers; yes, you who think you are too important for such an offering, you who are squirming at being addressed so directly, you who are accustomed to having a lawyer or an assistant or a wife handle messy things for you.

The Company has never made a profit. The Company went to Hollywood five years ago and had dinner with Barbra Streisand and slept in a mansion and had a button beside his bed direct to the Beverly Hills police. The Company came back to a roach-infested bungalow in Texas. The Company can only produce what you are seeing, just words, hot little clumps of breath, not words for Barbra Streisand and Clint Eastwood, only words for your insignificant ear, fellow risk taker.

The Company wants you to open your wallet.

The Company possesses no outline, no blueprints, no long-term plans.

The Company cannot provide any documentation for the process by which one sentence leads to another.

The Company has already lost everything once. It reorganized in 1979 and is now lean and desperate. The Company no longer possesses the facility to be ingratiating for profit, but it will, on occasion, be generous and friendly.

The Company considers you its only hope. This trust is the greatest risk of all.

Blood Relatives

This was one of my nightmares. A black man would come into my great-uncle's dim and silent house to pay his rent. While Uncle Jake was slowly printing out a receipt for $65 in crumpled bills the black man would spot my uncle's floor safe peeping out from behind the bedroom door. There was nobody else in the house and no close neighbors, only a vacant lot on either side. The tenant might figure that the old bald man was about done for anyway, so what the hell. The Negro would pull out a switchblade, cut my great-uncle ear to ear, pick up his receipt, and head for the safe.

I'm not particularly afraid of blacks. I think of the murderer as a black because Jake's entire business is conducted with them. He owns run-down houses and most of his tenants are colored. Because he doesn't drive, they bring their rents to his house. In New York you might call him a slumlord; in Muskegon he is just an old man who owns some undesirable property.

From the time I was sixteen and got my license I would drive my grandma to Muskegon every Sunday to visit her brother Jake. It was a forty-mile drive each way and I liked to put as many miles as possible on my Impala convertible.

The first time that I drove her in we went to the beach, where the two of them sat on a park bench in the shade and watched the Lake Michigan waves break. While I was carrying Cokes to them from the pavilion my grandma turned to me and said, "Watch out for the neegairs." These were a group of teenagers playing a rough basketball game on the cement court about ten feet behind the bench. I almost dropped the Cokes. Before I made it all the way to the bench, Jake corrected her. "You ought to call them darkies, they like that better."

Now this is not Atlanta, Georgia, around the turn of the century. I'm talking about Muskegon, Michigan, in about 1967. If you don't know Michigan very well, Muskegon is like saying Gary, Indiana, or Harlem. And Jake deals with black people every day and my grandma has been in the United States since right after World War I, and they're saying this in front of me, a high school junior who goes to an integrated school.

"You can't talk like that," I whispered, making sure that the basketball players hadn't already heard us. "You can't say 'neegairs,' and 'darkies' is just as bad. Don't even say 'shvartzers.' They understand that too. Call them black people or don't call them anything at all."

But they didn't listen to me about blacks any more than they did about other things. I was careful never to sit them near the basketball court again, but now and then one of the few words from the back seat that I understood was 'shvartzer.' All the way to Muskegon my grandma would sit back there silent as a stone. But as soon as her brother Jake got into the car the two of them would go at it, nonstop, in fast Yiddish. To me it all sounded like the names of Russian cities. I listened to the top 40 and cruised through town for an hour or so, then I headed for the beach in the summer or the L. C. Walker Arena on cold days. In the arena they sat on folding chairs and watched people ice skate. In the late afternoon we went to the Dairy Queen, where Jake bought us soft ice cream in the summer and hot tea in the winter. And all the time, in the car, at the beach, at the Walker

Arena, at the Dairy Queen, all the time they kept jabbering away in fast Yiddish. They didn't pay any attention to me or to anybody else who came along. Jake, who lived in Muskegon for maybe forty years, naturally knew lots of people. Someone would come over to say hello and Jake would maybe say a quick "How are you?" and then go right back to fast Yiddish with Grandma. No excuse me's, nothing. Most of the time I didn't even sit near them. I just walked around the beach or the arena, checking out the girls, and when my patience ran out I headed them toward the car.

I've told Jake lots of times that I don't like the way he ignores people to talk exclusively to Grandma, and he just ignores me too. I also don't like his change purse. The man owns maybe a half million dollars in property and he always carries exact change: 88 cents here, 43 cents there; you name it, he has it. All in that little striped coin purse, and he takes the coins out one at a time. It can take him a couple of minutes to pay for the Dairy Queens. He stands aside near the toothpick dispenser and counts out the change. The cashier knows him and doesn't mind, but it drives me up the wall. I bought him a new Rolf's wallet with a built-in coin purse so he would at least avoid the zippering, but he only used it for paper money. In the coin pocket he wadded up cash register receipts so he could deduct the sales tax. He also put green stamps in. The coins stayed in his old zippered purse.

Grandma did queer things too. She painted her toenails with Mercurochrome and wrapped her left knee in a big flannel rag to keep it warm, but at least none of this showed.

Still, the coin purse is a tiny thing compared to the safe. I don't know where he got it or how long it's been there. He keeps it in the bedroom, covered by a dingy gray vinyl tablecloth with red flowers on it. You can see the dark gray safe right through the vinyl. It's about three feet by two feet. He uses the top of it as a nightstand for his hairbrush, his glasses, and his teeth. And I don't really know what he keeps in it either. My great-uncle is no fool. He has a lot of money, and he keeps abreast of interest rates. You wouldn't think he would just let money lie around in a safe. But it's possible, because, even though he uses them, he does hate the banks. In 1933 he lost all the money he had in the Ravenna Bank. In the same year he spent two weeks in the county jail because a tenant in one of his houses was making bootleg whiskey and they mistakenly arrested Uncle Jake. "The bankers took eleven thousand dollars from me and none of them went to jail." He told me this every time I mentioned the safe and how dangerous it was to keep it in the house. I honestly didn't care about the money; I just didn't want anyone to kill him trying to get at it. Sometimes he told me that he kept no money in it. Other times he gave me that faraway look behind his bifocals and didn't answer.

I tried to be reasonable. "Look, Uncle Jake," I said, "look out your window. Across the street from you is a McDonald's. How many times have they been robbed?"

"Every year at least once. But they never shot anybody."

"OK. And a half block down Pine Street is the Liberty Loan Company. When was the last time they were robbed?"

"In July, I think. They get the loan company all the time."

"And in your house, don't you have poor black people coming in every few days to pay rent?"

"Sometimes every day."

"And what do these people think when they see a little old man alone in the house with a floor safe."

"They don't see it. I keep the bedroom closed up."

"Well, suppose they do see it. Haven't lots of your tenants been in jail?"

He smiles and reminds me that he was in jail too.

"Jake, it's not funny. People know you're old and alone and you have a lot of cash. Someday, a desperate person is liable to kill you to get into that safe."

"If they kill me they'll never get in."

"Uncle Jake," I told him, "what you do is your own business but that safe is like taking out a big sign advertising for people to rob you."

But when I got preachy he ignored me in a hurry, just like Grandma did. The two of them didn't know much about modern life, but when I tried to explain everyday things like what a radio wave is or what the chances are for life on other planets, the kind of thing I'm interested in, they just turned off. My grandma said something like, "In America they make a party every time the cat farts," and Jake just looked at the sky. His bifocals distort the tiny red lines of his eyes. He can sit there a long time ignoring you like that.

It's hard to know what he's thinking about when he sits there quietly behind his bifocals. Probably his houses or his money, because he usually comes out of his silence by saying something like, "Someday, Max, you'll be a rich man. It's all for you."

This makes me feel bad for both of us. Then all he talks about is a bunch of old houses that seem worthless to me. I hate to think that he is denying himself on account of my future.

"You're a rich man now, Uncle Jake. Enjoy yourself a little. Take a vacation. Go to Miami. Go to Israel."

"I can't go away and leave my house."

"You mean you can't go away and leave your safe."

Behind the bifocals again. The safe is rock bottom. Whatever it means to him must be something like religion is to most people. They just believe in it and don't want you to talk them out of it.

II

It turned out that I was concerned about the wrong person. My grandma, who lived with us and had good care and love, had a stroke one day out of the blue. She lingered for three months at home, but she was not herself. She said only disconnected things about events and people in the Russian towns nobody knew. While she was dying, Jake took a Greyhound bus in to see her twice a week. He would stand near the hospital bed we had rented for her and listen to her slow Yiddish. He would rarely answer. It didn't seem like the same language I used to hear in the back seat of the Impala. The slowness made it seem very decent, almost like a poem. Jake kept his hat on the whole time as if he was afraid that she might die while he was there next to her and he would have to go immediately into a Hebrew prayer for the dead.

One day, a few weeks before Grandma died, while I was in the bedroom with them and Grandma was asleep, Jake handed me a small slip of paper. I read his careful printing. He had never learned English longhand.

37 to the right, twice left to aught. Three times to the right stopping on 9 once, to the left on 5 . . .

It was a long series. I had never known a combination more complicated than a three-digit school locker or bicycle lock. He put his arm around me.

"Someday you'll need this. When I die you can get right in there without worrying about lawyers and estate taxes and everything."

I memorized the combination while we sat in the room listening to my grandma's heavy breathing that ended in a soft whistle. The next day, I put the combination in a safety deposit box at the bank near our house. The little slip of paper looked as if it didn't belong in a strongbox, just as Jake's thick safe didn't seem to belong in his small and dusty house.

III

Well, after my grandma died I still came to see Jake on Sundays, partly out of habit, partly because I was his heir, and I guess partly because I liked him too. Only it wasn't the same. He sat in the front seat with me and we both listened to the top 40. No more fast Yiddish, no more "neegairs." We didn't even have a taste for Dairy Queens when it was just the two of us and without much to say to one another. We both missed her an awful lot, and instead of stopping at the beach or the ice rink we just drove around Muskegon County. Jake pointed out things like some of his acreage in Section 60, or some of his houses in Muskegon Heights. He had the behind-the-bifocals look until we came to his land or his houses, and then he would wake up and tell me how much it was worth.

"You ought to write this down," he said. "Someday it will be yours. I'm seventy-eight."

I believed it when he told me how much some of these old houses were worth, but I couldn't imagine me ever going around to visit them on my own or collecting rent from the black people, so I just told him the truth.

"Uncle Jake, I'll sell those damn houses as fast as I can if you leave them to me."

It looked as if this bothered him, but I couldn't tell for sure. Then one Sunday while we were near a dilapidated house in the Heights, my Uncle Jake said, "Max, let's stop here for a while."

"I'm not going in there," I said, "not if you pay me."

"OK, you wait in the car."

I didn't like doing that either because it was such a crummy neighborhood, but I agreed because I didn't want him to think I was a chicken. He came out in a few minutes with a big black fellow about twenty and said, "This is Eugene, he's a good boy." Eugene smiled. The two of them got into the back seat and Jake seemed a lot less melancholy than at any time since before my grandma got sick. He even said, "Why don't we drive down to the beach?" but I didn't feel like killing the rest of the day so we just stopped in the Heights and I took Eugene home after about a half hour.

The next Sunday when I got to Jake's I found Eugene there on the porch steps, and every Sunday after that too.

"He's a carpenter," Jake said, "and Eugene and me are a good pair, eh, Eugene? I've got the old houses and Eugene here knows how to fix 'em. Right, Eugene?"

"Right on, Mr. S."

Of course I resented Eugene's being with us. He didn't have a driver's license so I just continued to be the chauffeur while he took my grandma's place in the back seat and we started going to the old places, the beach and the ice rink and the Dairy Queen, plus a new one that Eugene suggested, Jemima's, where he ate soul food while Jake and I drank tea. And Jake paid the bill. This is how I could tell he liked Eugene, because $1.80 or so is quite a bit for Jake to part with for the sake of good manners.

When I asked him about it he wouldn't say much, only that Eu-

gene saved him a lot of money, being very good at carpentry and
nonunion.

"What do you pay him?" I asked. Jake pretended not to hear me
so I asked again.

"We have a deal worked out," Jake finally said. "Eugene's people
are way behind on their house payments, over a year behind, so
Eugene is working some of it off for them."

"You mean you're not paying him anything."

"He's got a roof over his head and he can't get another job now
he'll be going to the army pretty soon. Eugene and me, we get along
first class. We're both satisfied."

For a few months after he took up with Eugene I continued
visiting, but finally I couldn't take it anymore. Eugene wanted to go
to the roller rink instead of the Walker Arena when the ice skating
season began, and it was no more Dairy Queens, but always
Jemima's or Brother Adolph's, and Eugene started putting away a
few beers too. Some of his black friends would come over and give
my Uncle Jake five and even ask him to play the pinballs. I drank
hot tea and felt uncomfortable, but I understood damn well what my
cagey great-uncle was up to. He had himself a slave laborer all week
so on Sundays he buttered the boy up. Why not? Sunday was a lonely
day for Jake, and this kept Eugene happy.

"Uncle Jake," I said, "if you keep up with Eugene I'm not coming
here every Sunday. I've got other things to do, you know."

He looked at me and shrugged. "Eugene's a good worker. Fastest
carpenter I ever had, and a good plumber too."

"Do you want to spend your time with your nephew or with your
laborer, Uncle Jake? That's what it comes down to."

He looked away from me and then he looked right back at me.

"Max, Eugene's a good boy and valuable to me. You be a good
boy too."

"I'll be good, but not in Muskegon, not on Sundays, not anymore."

And I didn't go back or even call for a month.

IV

When I stopped going to Muskegon on Sundays I started to worry about the money. It's true I was his closest relative and he had liked me since I was a baby. Still, he had two other great-nephews in Chicago and, on his late wife's side, sisters-in-law who were poor and trying to send kids through college. He told me several times that Sarah (whom I barely remembered) had asked him to help out her family after she was gone. She had a weak heart and spent all her time crocheting. Jake still has crocheted headrests on all his furniture and a crocheted tablecloth that you know had to have taken her hundreds of hours. She died before they had television in Muskegon.

One Sunday when I was just cruising around with nothing to do, I said to myself, Are you going to pass up thousands in cash because you're jealous of a carpenter? I also missed Jake without knowing why, and I headed down I-96 toward Muskegon. When I got to his place it was about 3 P.M. and Cadillacs were parked all over. A black man answered the door.

"Hey, Mr. S., there's a dude here says he's your nephew." From the doorway I could see Uncle Jake coming out of the kitchen. He was wearing a green crocheted vest and looked pretty happy.

"C'mon in, Max. These are some of Eugene's friends. They just came over for the afternoon. It's a little party." I was so scared that I shook. He had a safe full of money and was entertaining a roomful of street blacks. I hesitated but went in. There were about six men and a few women all dressed fancy and looking very out of place on Jake's undusted 1940ish furniture. They were admiring his Victrola, one of the original automatic models, and trying to play some of his 78s. All he had were a few Hebrew melodies and some comic albums. They were listening to Mickey Katz singing "Herring Boats Are Coming." "Herring boats, brother," said one of the spades, "herring boats is comin'," and walked around the room giving everyone a little skin. There was also a record of my Bar Mitzvah reading and a speech I gave about Noah's ark. When one of them put it on I decided to leave the house, but I realized that they didn't know who I was and what would any of it mean to them? My cracking thirteen-year-old voice sounded out in Hebrew. The tale of Noah and his two-by-two's. They sat around nodding as if it were Nina Simone. Eugene poured new drinks for everyone from a big bottle of Gallo. I walked over to Jake and nudged him into the kitchen alone.

"You've gone nuts, haven't you, Uncle Jake?"

"Don't be afraid, Max. These are good boys, my work crew. We have to remodel completely a house on Summit Street. Eugene got these boys together. In one week they did—you wouldn't believe what they did. If I was younger I'd go into the construction business. These boys could build you a city."

"Are you paying them?"

Jake got angry this time. "Of course I'm paying them. Don't you know there's a minimum wage?" He walked into the living room, where my high gravelly voice was now discoursing in English upon Shem, Ham, and Japheth. I didn't remember any of it.

"Noah had three sons," the thirteen-year-old me was saying, "and from them the whole earth was peopled. But this man Noah who was a good man in the eyes of the Lord was still a drunkard."

"Amen," said a couple of Jake's crew. "Amen."

"And Noah planted a vineyard and drank of the wine and became drunk. The lesson is not that Noah was weak, but that any man may succumb."

I remembered "succumb." It was hard to say that word. A rabbi whose name I didn't remember had written the speech for me.

"Any man may succumb to temptation, to ease, to the simple pleasure of relaxation. After all, who in history ever needed to relax more than Noah needed to relax?"

"Amen, brother, amen. Herring boats is comin'."

"Yet the lesson is that Noah shouldn't have relaxed when he did, because he brought evil into the lives of his children. Parents cannot relax completely until they know their children's education has a good moral foundation. That is why I thank my parents on this day for what they have already given me in love and in education. But most of all I thank them for not relaxing now that the flood of my Bar Mitzvah is over. I thank them for continuing my Hebrew education beyond this day. They have learned from Noah's mistake, and it is learning from past errors that makes any man great. Noah or you or I."

"Amen. Amen, brother."

"That you?" One of the girls was pointing at me, and I didn't dare lie.

"I was just thirteen then. That's a religious ceremony."

"You a preacher or somethin'?"

"Shit, no. Hardly been in one of our churches since that day. I didn't really promise to go on with that stuff. They wrote the speech for me."

"That's too bad, man, you messed yourself up real good. Is he a mess, Mr. S., this nephew of yours, is he a mess?"

"Max is a good boy." Jake smiled.

I was grateful to him. She had long sharp fingernails and heavy perfume.

We all listened to "Herring Boats Are Coming" with bagels and lox and amened that one too. Jake and I both took a little bit of wine. Everyone was friendly to me except Eugene. Jake must have told him why I had stopped coming.

At a little after four they all left for Brother Adolph's and took Eugene with them.

"Uncle Jake," I said when we were alone again, "I don't know what I can say to you. It seems like yesterday I was telling you and Grandma not to call them niggers and darkies, and now you're a regular soul brother. I'm not criticizing you for it, Jake, I just don't think it's safe."

"It's OK. They all live in my houses. I know their parents. Eugene got everyone together. You can't pay union wages. Without them I'd have to let the city board up my property. What would I do then?"

"You could retire. You're seventy-eight years old."

"You retire," he said. "I've finally got a good crew of boys and plenty of work for them. I bought a used car and Alex fixed it up and drives me around."

"But they're not your kind of people, Uncle Jake."

"Your grandma was the last of my kind of people. Everyone else is strangers to me."

I felt kind of bad because I knew he meant it. "Me too?"

"You too," he said as he slipped my Bar Mitzvah album back into its dust jacket.

V

The afternoon of the party was the last I saw of my great-uncle Jake for a long time. By then I was through with junior college and I joined the naval reserve to avoid being drafted. This took me to Norfolk, Virginia, for six months. I sent Jake a couple of postcards and now and then, when I would be on a cruise with a group of blacks, I would think of Jake and wonder what he was up to, but my life was too busy for me to worry about him. When I came home it took me a couple of weeks to get settled and find a good job. When I asked how Uncle Jake was doing, my folks said they hadn't heard from him in months. My grandma and I were the only ones who liked him, so I wasn't surprised that nobody had kept in touch. I decided to go to Muskegon that Sunday and surprise him. I wore my uniform so he could see how I looked. He had been in the Russian army when he was seventeen and had a picture of himself in uniform that I always liked.

He wasn't home so I waited in the car for a while; then I went to the corner to ask Mr. Robinson, who sometimes drove Jake around town, if he knew when my uncle would be back.

"Jake's in the hospital," Mr. Robinson told me. "Been there since Wednesday with a real bad cold that they say took to pneumonia."

I shot over to St. Mary's Hospital, remembering the sound of my grandma's breathing. Jake was in a private room and under an oxygen tent. He looked pale and had about a three-day growth of white beard. While he slept I noticed how deep the caverns of his nostrils were. This I had noticed on Grandma too. It looked as if the

nostrils became big and deep while the rest of the body was shrink-
ing. You could see almost all the way up to the eyes. I was already
imagining another painful death marked by slow disconnected Yiddish sentences when a nurse woke Jake for his medicine. He gave
me a weak smile and waved.

"You'll be OK, Uncle Jake," I said. "They'll take good care of
you here."

"You bet we will," the nurse said. "He knows that already, don't
you, honey."

I followed her into the hall.

"That Mr. Shapiro is such a cute little fellow," she said.

"How is he?" I asked. "I mean, is he going to recover? I've just
come back from the Reserves. I haven't seen him in six months."

"Oh, he'll be fine. Of course you'll have to ask Dr. Conmel, I
haven't seen his whole record, but he's doing so much better. His
temperature's almost down to normal and the oxygen is clearing him
out real well. He's a good man for his age. He gets lots of Negro
visitors," she said. "In fact, I think you're the first white person
who's been up to see him."

"The blacks work for him," I said.

"Well, they certainly are loyal. The first night when his cough was
pretty bad, a young colored man and a girl stayed here all night
wiping the phlegm from his lips. It was really very touching. They
wanted to donate blood for him. When I told them that Mr. Shapiro
didn't need any transfusions, they both went over and gave some
blood anyway. You don't find white people like that these days."

"I'm his nephew," I said, "a blood relative."

"That's interesting. Well, I'm sure he's going to be just fine in a
few days. The doctor makes rounds at about ten if you want to see
him in the morning."

I sat in the waiting room while Jake slept. The hospital cots, the
constant movement of people in the hallways, and the loudspeaker
system all reminded me of the S.S. Arkansas that I was going to tell
Jake about that afternoon. Because I had nothing else to do, I took
a quick ride over to the Dairy Queen for a Coke. It was the only time
I had ever been in the place alone. First it had been the three of us,

then Jake and I, and for a few weeks Jake and Eugene and I. I paid quickly and picked my change off the rubber mat on which Jake used to carefully count out his coins.

I got back to the hospital just as Eugene and Alex were going into his room. They were in work clothes even though it was Sunday. Eugene recognized me and nodded. We all went quietly into the room. Before I could stop him, Eugene lifted up the oxygen tent and tapped my Uncle Jake on the shoulder. Jake looked up.

"Summit Street plumbing all done, Mr. S. Hot water running like hell."

Jake broke into a big smile.

"Sweet Eugene," Alex said, "he's done it up real good. Them dudes can move on in tomorrow."

"Wonderful, boys, wonderful." Jake's voice sounded pretty good. Before I could get in a goodbye the nurse came in and put the plastic tent down. I just waved and said I'd be back tomorrow.

It was Tuesday night, though, before I could get back. I was tired after a long day at work and only went because I would have felt guilty if I didn't go.

The room was brightly lit. There was no longer an oxygen tent. Jake was sitting in the bed propped up by pillows. He had shaved and his skin looked pink and healthy. Eugene and Alex and a girl were standing around the bed. The girl was arranging some carnations on the bedside table.

"I'm feeling fine," Jake said. "And the boys have finished up all the houses, Max, even the condemned ones. Without them I'd have had to board everything up."

He drank some soup through a bent straw from a glass the girl handed to him.

"They kept me in business, Eugene, Alex, and the boys."

I was so happy to see Uncle Jake looking healthy and in such good spirits that I didn't even resent Eugene. I walked over to where he stood underneath the cross and shook his hand.

"Congratulations, Eugene," I said. "You've done a good job."

Eugene held my hand and drew me close to him. He whispered

in my ear, "Thirty-seven to the right, twice left to aught, three times to the right stopping on nine once, to the left on five . . ."

While the numbers sank in, Eugene put a light kiss on my cheek.

I looked back at my great-uncle Jake, radiant now among the white pillows, on his way to recovery from pneumonia and full of hope for the future of his remodeled houses.

"Darkies," he said to me, "are the best help, when you get good ones."